The prince's w[...] grew, even as h[...] even-keeled, as [...] weather rather than marriage.

"I need a particular kind of wife, of which you fit the bill, and you want to come with me to Hayat. It will be a business arrangement."

A business arrangement?

The words rattled around Rita's mind. Did she want a business arrangement for a marriage?

As if summoned in answer, her mother's long-ago words rose in Rita's mind. *Marriage is always an arrangement. It is an arrangement in which two people have to wake up every day and work with each other to make a good life. No matter how it starts, the arrangement is the same, and it's hard enough that, love or no love, it falls apart almost as much as it doesn't.*

Rita hadn't thought about that conversation in years, hadn't even realized she remembered it until now.

Once again, she was looking at the prospect of marriage—but this time it was a business arrangement.

And her dad had been wrong after all.

Someone *had* asked to marry her.

And not just any someone, but an honest-to-goodness real-life prince.

Pregnant Princesses

When passionate nights lead to unexpected heirs

Vincenzo, Rafael, Zeus and Jahangir are princes bound for life by their ruthless quests to rebel against their tyrannical fathers. But their plans will be outrageously upended when forbidden nights with forbidden princesses leave them facing the most shocking of consequences...and convenient marriages that spark much more than scandal!

Marcella Bell

HIS BRIDE WITH
TWO ROYAL SECRETS

HARLEQUIN®
PRESENTS™

Recycling programs
for this product may
not exist in your area.

ISBN-13: 978-1-335-56958-5

His Bride with Two Royal Secrets

Copyright © 2022 by Marcella Bell

For questions and comments about the quality of this book, please contact us at CustomerService@Harlequin.com.

Harlequin Enterprises ULC
22 Adelaide St. West, 41st Floor
Toronto, Ontario M5H 4E3, Canada
www.Harlequin.com

Printed in U.S.A.

rcella Bell is an avid reader, a burgeoning
der, and a corvid and honeybee enthusiast
more interests than hours in the day. As a late
omer and a yogini, Marcella is drawn to stories
t showcase love's incredible power to inspire
sformation—whether they take place in the
t landscapes of the West or imagined palaces
d exotic locales. When not writing or wrangling
multigenerational household and three dogs,
loves to hear from readers! To reach out, keep
or check in, visit marcellabell.com.

Books by Marcella Bell

Harlequin Presents

The Queen's Guard

Stolen to Wear His Crown
His Stolen Innocent's Vow
Pregnant After One Forbidden Night

Visit the Author Profile page
at Harlequin.com for more titles.

To Innovation and Hope

CHAPTER ONE

ᴊᴀɢ ꜱᴛʀᴏᴅᴇ ɪɴᴛᴏ the bright, vast garage in time to witness a dark-haired woman wearing an obnoxious lime-green jumpsuit reach out to delicately caress his priceless vintage Ferrari GTO.

The Ferrari, which gleamed in glacier-blue perfection, rested atop a round white platform beneath a bright spotlight.

The woman's hand upon it was gentle and lingering, like that of a lover's cupping of the curved hip of their beloved.

Something unfamiliar and powerful jolted through Jag's body at the sight of it, though he remained where he stood.

Hard or soft, the pressure of her touch didn't matter.

She did not have permission to touch his car.

"Mmm…" she purred, unaware of Jag's presence, her voice lingering on the sound with the same sensuality with which she handled his vehicle. "Practically perfect," she continued in a low, throaty voice. "In every way. It's an outrage

that I don't get to keep you all to myself. On
know how to take care of something as preci
and rare as you."

Her words were slightly breathless, each :
lable heavy and erotic, as if she and the car
isted in a private world of their own.

Jag swallowed, his hand clenching at his s
so that he didn't involuntarily lift it to accept
invitation that he logically knew she was not
fering to him.

But maybe by proxy?

Shaking the outrageous thought out of |
head, he blinked slowly, intentionally unclenc
ing his hand at his side.

That he was here at all, at the very weste
edge of the United States—as opposed to atten
ing to any number of the many interests he h.
as Crown Prince of the independent emirate
Hayat—was absolutely ridiculous.

To have arrived in time to discover a stran;
woman pawing his precious jewel was utter
unconscionable.

Equally offensive was the fact that the car w.
the one thing left in Jag's world that could be use
to manipulate him. And while NECTAR did n
directly control that, he'd certainly revealed t
the world that it was true.

Which was, naturally, the point that offende
Jag the most.

Manipulation by means of the heart was the thing he hated most in all of creation.

Through restricting the output of his love, doling it out rarely and only to those in command of their own security forces with at least a modicum of demonstrated martial acuity, he had thought himself to have been thoroughly cured of that particular weakness, and for a very long time now.

But he had been utterly immovable on the decision to travel all this way—against his better judgment and adviser's wishes—for the humble pleasure of having his own property back.

Adding insult to injury, he had done so at the demand of a man whom literally no one had ever met, no one could physically describe, and now, only Jag knew the location of. Well, now Jag and his security team. Obviously, he had not walked into an American blind spot without a contingency and retrieval plan. He was too important for that. That would have been irresponsible.

But at least the beauty that shone before him was worth it—beauty of the four-wheeled variety, he mentally insisted.

Though her back remained to him, he could sense that the woman, too, was beautiful, as well as appreciate the tantalizing view of her generously rounded rear end and shapely thighs and calves.

But he didn't have time for the woman. He w
here for the car.

While Jag was happy to play light and car
free in the company of the few individuals
loved in this world, and to become a master s
ducer when he needed to let off a little stear
since stepping into his role as Crown Prince an
officially instituting his plan to bring his fath
to ruin, his playboy prince persona had been p
firmly behind him.

His people wanted their prince to be a whole
some family role model and, to the best of h
ability, he would give his people what the
wanted—both because a good leader put th
needs of his people above his own, and becaus
he needed to be popular if he was going to over
throw his father without bloodshed.

For not the first time, Jag deliberately pulled
his attention away from the curvy creature o
flesh before him and returned it to his angel or
four wheels, drawing in a long breath as he did
it, and exhaling only once he got there.

The car was pristine. Possibly in the top tier
of most stunning objects he had ever laid his
eyes on.

And there would be plenty of time to admire
it, and women, when he returned to Hayat.

But between planning the largest international
event that Hayat had ever seen and launching the
final phase of his plan to oust his father from the

one, there was not a lot of room in his sched-
e for leisurely exchanges with reclusive auto-
otive geniuses.

There was simply too much at stake.

Even if it was true that NECTAR had never
oken directly with a single client—Jag in-
uded—until demanding to meet with Jag face-
-face.

But the success of Jag's exhibition depended
pon that car, and the success of his coup de-
ended on the success of the exhibition, so here
e was, waiting for NECTAR while a strange
oman pawed his prize.

And on that matter, the clock was ticking. In
ruth, both he and his car had bigger concerns
han smudges and fingerprints, and it was past
ime they get on with them.

Clearing his throat, surprised at the thickness
hat had accumulated there while he'd watched
he mechanic, Jag managed to get out a low, more
or less smooth and ominous, "Careful, there,"
hough his voice still caught as it exited his throat.
Strengthening and carrying more of the original
remonstrative disdain than he had intended, he
added, "I'm sure your employer wouldn't appreciate you smudging the finish."

But rather than startling and pulling her hand
back like a thief caught in the act, the woman instead went absolutely still, her hand remaining
firmly affixed to the side of his vehicle.

And as she turned to face him, he was forced to admit that she was a risk to him of the oldest and most potent variety.

She was gorgeous.

Her hair was dark, and glossy, and thick.

Her skin was bright and clear, an umber tone that glowed, silky, smooth and warmth.

Her dusky-rose-colored lips matched the rest of her full and expressive beauty, while her nose was well shaped and adorable and her eyes large and brown.

If she weren't dressed up in mechanic's gear, she would have looked like a princess from a fairy tale.

Their eyes locked.

Her straight eyebrows drew together, the deep color of her lush lips pressing into a line.

And from the light burning in her dark brown eyes, it was clear that she had the audacity to be offended by *him*. *She* had been the one fondling *his* car.

"Prince Jahangir, I presume," she said, as if *his* property were not the subject of their conversation and his title were simply a superfluous adjective.

Nothing in what she said neared an apology, nor an explanation, nor anything remotely remonstrative. In fact, there was not an ounce of regret in her voice.

If anything, she sounded as if she were dis-

ointed at his behavior, and not just that. Her
ce also made it clear that she was additionally
appointed with herself—for expecting better
him.

t had been so long since anyone had used a
e like that on him that it took the Prince a mo-
nt to place it.

Only his mother had ever spoken to him like
at. *And where had a thought like that come
m?* Shaking his head, he pushed the memory
ay, rather than let it linger.

"Indeed," he responded, instead. "I am here
retrieve my vehicle at NECTAR's...*request.*"

The woman laughed, and it broke through the
itation on her face. Lifting her lips, her glori-
s eyes crinkling at the corners, she appeared
emanate her own light, though Jag knew that
uldn't be true. It had to be because she stood
neath the car's spotlight.

Jag stared, unable to quite adjust to the watt-
ge of her smile as well as a bit taken aback by
e whole situation itself.

If he wasn't mistaken, she was laughing at him.

As her laughter died down, though she re-
ained smiling, she said, "I'm NECTAR. In peron, though, people usually call me Rita."

As though he had not been thrown for a loop,
ag verified, "*You* are NECTAR?"

Meeting his eye, which was a feat he had long
go given up on expecting of most people, the

woman said, "I sure hope so. Otherwise you j
paid the wrong person a lot of money for this c
Not to mention entrusted a car worth its weig
in gold to the wrong person."

Jag blinked once, then nodded as if the i
formation were to be expected when it entire
was not.

NECTAR was a woman.

NECTAR was a beautiful woman. Possibly t
most beautiful woman he had ever met.

And her tone was chastising.

The facts that she had been the only individu
he'd seen on the premises, apart from the drive
she'd sent to pick him up from the airport, an
had had her hands all over a car that most king
and queens would be afraid to touch, should hav
made it all obvious, he realized now.

As had the fact that she had not been intimi
dated by him in the least.

And why would she be? He might be a crow
prince, but so were most of her clients. An
hadn't she just successfully demanded that h
jump at her command?

Jag said, "I assume that's my car?"

Rita moistened her lips, leaving them plump
and glistening, and said, a bit breathlessly, "It':
the only 1962 Ferrari GTO that's ever come
through my garage."

There were those who said it was the rares
car in the world.

And the purists of the world would decry that
had ruined it by ordering the conversion.

The two of them, however, knew that her work
d made a unicorn into a legend.

"It's lovely that you appreciate its rarity," Jag
id, unable to stop the bit of humor threading
to his voice. Clearing his throat before he spoke
ain, and straightening his already upright pos-
re, he added, "However, I imagine that there
as a greater purpose to your summoning me
re than a discussion of that. Otherwise, I'm
raid I need to take it home now."

To his utter shock, she held her palms up, with
firm, "No."

"Excuse me?" Jag asked, apparently still ca-
able of being surprised despite the fact that she
ad already proved exceptionally bold.

"Wait—"

"I can't," he said, and there was some real
hame in that. But kingdoms came before be-
uiling women. They had to when people's daily
ives depended upon the behavior of a handful
f individuals. "It is an honor to own one of the
vorld's most precious automobiles, and an even
reater one yet, that it is also the work of such a
enowned engineer as yourself. However, I can-
ot linger nor offer any more than my apprecia-
ion, compliments and the substantial amount of
noney I've paid you for the privilege."

She disabused him of the notion that she was

looking for more money, however, with the n
thing she said.

"Take me with you," she blurted out, the wo
running together in her rush to get them out
heard about the exhibition, I know what you
planning to do, and you need me around to ma
sure it happens. If you're going to succeed,
car has to be perfect at all times. No one can ke
it that way other than me."

Jag froze. She had no idea what he was pla
ning to do with his exhibition. She had like
read the official marketing materials about t
exhibition and thought it was all about the ca

"And what's in it for you?" he asked, voice lo

"I have to be there. It's the best place I c
showcase my work, my talent. The place to ma
the connections that I need to in order to achie
my long-term goals. The most important nam
in electric vehicles will be there, so I have to
there, too. The connections I could make…yo
wouldn't even need to acknowledge me. I ju
need to be in the room where it happens," sl
pleaded earnestly.

It made sense.

Of course she would want to be a part of it–
she was the world's leading engineer when
came to electric vehicles.

But electric futures were not the only thin
his exhibition was about, and she had no ide

he kind of danger and intrigue that boiled beneath the surface.

Only his close friends, the total of whom he
could count on one hand, knew just what his
plans were. There was no conceivable reason to
add babysitting a strange and alluring woman
into that mix.

Except for the fact that she was right about
the car.

And that she was alluring and strange and
beautiful.

But most importantly, the car.

It did have to be perfect, for every moment
of the exhibition. And not just for the race, but
for the countless showcases and press events and
demonstrations as well. Old cars, as well as con-
verted cars, were high-maintenance under the
best of conditions. A weeklong showcase of the
power, range and capacity of electric vehicles,
starring a vehicle that had been born in the same
year as his mother, rest her soul, was not exactly
the best of conditions.

NECTAR guaranteed lifelong service for all
of his—or rather, her—vehicles, but that service
required to and fro international transport and
resulted in intolerable waiting times.

Her offer made absolute sense.

But still, Jag refused. "Absolutely not."

He owed it to her to protect her—even if it was
just against her own recklessness.

Honestly, what was she thinking?

She didn't know the first thing about Haya she didn't speak the language and, most impotantly, she had no idea what she was asking. Di she have no sense of self-preservation?

Probably not. Like most Americans, she probably believed that the world was wild and fre and full of desperate dreamers.

In Hayat, she would merely be another soul h was responsible for keeping safe and happy while simultaneously staging a coup.

But damn, she was right about the car.

His eyes found hers desperate, and he paused

For an instant her expression shuttered, and she took a deep breath. Then a layer of resolution settled over her.

On an exhale, she said, "I'll let you pick out a car from my personal fleet if you let me come."

Jag blinked.

She was beautiful and ingenuous and enigmatic, and he simply didn't have the time to take care of her while he dealt with his father.

But that was before she'd offered him a vehicle from her personal fleet, a sly voice inside reminded.

And there was the point she'd made about maintenance. And, as she was one of the world's foremost experts on electric cars, he could build her into the program, even this late in the game.

An idea was beginning to form in his mind.

His advisers had told him multiple times since his permanent return to Hayat that marriage would greatly boost his popularity. It was a step he had resisted, however, despite being willing to refrain from having public romantic associations, because he had not been willing to take the risk of making a woman his bride.

A marriage of convenience with a logical peer—a woman of high status, wealth and connections—was simply too big a risk, given his plans.

The kind of woman who would go into a partnership like that with open eyes would undoubtedly bring a level of honed cynicism that just wasn't a good idea to have around when one was planning a coup.

That left him with the alternative of pursuing and wooing, which he had neither the time nor the duplicity for.

He would not present himself as a genuine lover to a woman when he knew that was something he would never be.

He had learned long ago that love, affection and closeness were liabilities when one had a father like his. It would not be right to capture a heart that he had no intention of caring for and keeping.

And, of course, there was the matter of the vow that he and the three men he considered friends had made while still young foreign men doing a long stint in English boarding school.

Jag and his friends had done their damnedest to fight back at every step, and even making plans into the future, such as in their promise to one another that when the time came, they would each find the most unsuitable brides they could.

Vin, Rafael and even Zeus may have pushed the boundaries of their vow by falling into real love with their unsuitable brides, but each had met the terms without causing harm to their people.

Jag could do no less, particularly when a brilliant and beautiful opportunity knocked.

Bringing a thumb and forefinger to stroke his beard, Jag reconsidered Rita, otherwise known as NECTAR. She was equal parts famous and mysterious.

She had an eye for design and detail, a mind for engineering and complex systems, and in making demands of a powerful man she barely knew, had shown herself to be both dangerously bold and categorically reckless.

She was wealthy—if the fees she charged and her property were any indication—and charismatic. She was passionate about cars, as he was famous for being, and a leader in electric transportation at a time when he was leading Hayat into becoming a world leader in clean energy.

he made sense as much as the absurd plan
ning in his mind did not.

*nd she has a body that begs to be driven
ng with the face of a heavenly maiden, his
n internal recklessness pointed out—though
t point he ruthlessly pushed aside.

Her body and face were irrelevant insofar as
future of their relationship was to go.

He was not considering this outrageous idea
cause he wanted her.

He was considering it because as she was nei-
r a steely-eyed socialite nor a woman he had
fool into love, she was safe to bring into his
cle.

He didn't need her to be attractive.

He needed her to be a woman who wouldn't
ing shame to his nation or people while simul-
ncously posing no threat to his plans, nor any
k of emotional entanglement.

She was a lovely stranger with her own pre-
gatives, and as he'd encountered thus far, as
ansparent as a glass window, and, as genius
she was, when you boiled it down, she was a
echanic.

She was perfect.

She would get whatever it was that she wanted
get out of attending his exhibition, and he
ould gain in popularity without trouble, risk
wasted time.

If she were willing to agree to his terms, she

would get what she wanted, he would get k
car back, and, as the Lord had apparently cod
dinated it, get an added boost in public suppc
while at the same time fulfilling the terms
an agreement he'd made with his closest frien
when they'd been only hints of the men th
were today.

A wicked and decided grin lifted one side
his mouth and then the other.

Opening it to speak, Jag countered her offe
"A car, even one from the world-famous NEC
TAR's personal fleet, is nowhere near enoug
for the kind of inconvenience you're asking c
me. However, there is a condition upon which
would be willing to bring you along."

She swallowed, but she didn't look away, an
her voice was resolute and earnest when sh
promised him the world without knowing wha
it was. "Anything."

"Marry me."

CHAPTER TWO

"WH-WHAT?" RITA STAMMERED, the wind knocked ut of her as if she had taken a hit to the chest. Why?"

She had offered him a car, and he had asked or her hand in marriage instead. But this was no pen-air market, and they were not a buyer and eller haggling over the price of goods.

This was real life.

The Prince's wicked smile somehow grew, even as his tone remained even-keeled, as if they discussed the weather rather than marriage. "I need a particular kind of wife, of which you fit the bill, and you want to come with me to Hayat. It will be a business arrangement."

A business arrangement?

The words rattled around Rita's mind. Did she want a business arrangement for a marriage?

As if summoned in answer, her mother's long-ago words rose in Rita's mind.

Marriage is always an arrangement. It is an arrangement in which two people have to wake

up every day and work with each other to m
a good life. No matter how it starts, the arran
ment is the same, and it's hard enough that, l
or no love, it falls apart almost as much a
doesn't.

Rita hadn't thought about that conversati
in years, hadn't even realized she remember
it until now. Once again, she was looking at
prospect of marriage—but this time it was a bu
ness arrangement.

And her dad had been wrong after all.

Someone *had* asked to marry her.

And not just any someone, but an honest-t
goodness, real-life prince.

If he had not also been a client whom she
only just met and had spent less than an ho
with in her entire life, the situation could ha
been plucked straight out of a fairy tale.

"What kind of arrangement are we talkin
about here?" Rita asked, caution tingling in h
limbs.

Pressing his lips together, moistening them a
most effectively and seductively as if he'd licke
his lips, the Prince said, "Strictly business. Not
ing physical beyond presenting the image of
happy couple to the public."

The man who had just asked her to marry hin
was, without contest, the most compelling ma
she had ever seen in her life.

His nose was straight and true down the cen

er of his face. His eyebrows were thick and coal lack, an exact match to the gorgeous mane on is head and neatly trimmed facial hair that ramed his defined face and square jaw.

At the moment, his eyes glowed a glorious amber, his expression captivating her, willing her to hold contact.

Just the eyes alone had enough voltage to power her whole system.

And that wasn't even considering the way that his incredibly tall and broad body filled out the impeccable lines of his suit.

Had she ever used the word *impeccable* in the context of men's clothing before? She didn't think so.

While she struggled to return her inner world to any semblance of order, his gaze remained fixed upon hers like that of a hunter who moved silently and struck in the night.

His astounding irises were rich amber encircled in a deep brown ring and striped throughout with small streaks of equally dark brown.

The intensity of the glow that shone from within them was a reminder that although he had been gifted with a body that was more than enough to house all of that power, being caged only made it all the more desperate to escape.

And, for all intents and purposes, he'd just asked her to marry him.

But why had he asked her to marry him? If he

was looking for a business arrangement, w[...]
singled her out as the woman to make it with[...]

And did the answer matter?

"What's the catch?" Rita asked.

He swallowed, and she realized that he w[...]
just as caught in their stare as she was.

"Some women might consider marrying [...]
stranger all the catch they needed."

"Some women wouldn't think twice abo[...]
marrying a handsome and mysterious prince.[...]

Laughter flared in his eyes, though he onl[...]
released a chuckle. "Don't forget rich beyon[...]
limit."

Rita swallowed this time, and it wasn't just be[...]
cause there was something magnetic about hi[...]
awareness of his own power.

As NECTAR she had done well for hersel[...]
her years of struggle behind her now, but she wa[...]
far from living a life beyond limit—wasn't ever[...]
sure, really, if she knew what that meant.

"There has to be a catch," she insisted.

He inclined his head with respect. "In addition[...]
to marrying a stranger, you will be inheriting a[...]
ruthless tyrant for a father-in-law. Being my wife[...]
will keep you safe from him, but he, unfortunately, exists nonetheless."

Rita knew a thing or two about complicated
and tyrannical fathers.

"And you're not after anything physical?" she
queried.

Nodding, the Prince said, "I am, in fact, un-
uivocally rejecting anything physical. A phys-
l relationship would undermine what makes
is such a good arrangement."

"I'm not sure I'm clear on what makes this
ch a good arrangement."

"My people would like to see me married, but
m interested in neither a life partner nor a con-
lant. You can see how being up-front about that
ight turn prospects away. On the other hand,
would be disingenuous to pretend to be inter-
sted in a wife when, in reality, I am merely in
vant of one. An acquaintance with some com-
non ground and her own life, however, stands
ut to me as a solution. One that only works if
ve remember between the two of us that it is all
n act. Sex can complicate keeping that in mind.
o that end, I reiterate that there is not and never
vill be anything romantic about our arrangement.
This arrangement could work well for the two of
is for many reasons, but romance is not one of
hem," he said.

"I can see how marrying a stranger could make
it easier to maintain distance," she mused on the
thought. Taking it further, she asked, "So you're
proposing that we remain as close as we can to
strangers in matrimony for the rest of our, mostly
separate from the sounds of it, lives?"

The Prince's eyes once again danced with
humor. "Hardly," he said, as easy being inter-

rogated as he was tossing out proposals. "A few
years is all I expect, and then we can divorce like
normal modern royalty."

Something shuddered through Rita at the word
divorce, but she told herself she could handle that
stigma as well as she could handle the stigma of
having been disowned.

But she wouldn't be taken advantage of in the
process.

"What about a prenup?" she asked.

The Prince's eyes narrowed and cooled ever so
slightly, but he replied smoothly, "My assets will
be protected, I assure you. I had not taken you to
be the kind of individual I needed to protect them
from, however. Should I revise that opinion?"

Rita let out a short laugh, shaking her head.

All she cared about was her cars.

According to her family, cars were all she had
ever cared about.

But if she and the Prince were planning a marriage with an expiration date, she was getting it
down in writing that her babies stayed with her
when that date arrived.

"My private fleet is a collection of priceless
one-of-a-kind vehicles. How do I know this isn't
just some elaborate scheme to take them from
me?"

Just because he was wealthy beyond limit and
royal did not mean that he was above trickery.

For years now, Rita had worked among the rich

famous, and in those years and from those
ople, she had seen some of the most outrageous
empts to get more than their fair share out of
for free. Worse yet, were those who had out-
ht tried to steal from her.

Reluctant as she was to think cynically about
e people she met, as a young brown female
novator operating in mostly male-dominated
alms, Rita had learned that a vast majority of
e powerful men that she encountered were, at
e very least, going to try to intimidate her, and
at the only way to combat it was to look past
eir facades, speak clearly and firmly, and stand
o for herself.

The suspicious edge leaving him, the Prince's
es heated once again. "If you want one, I'll
ave one drawn up immediately, ensuring that
ery single one of your vehicles, sans the Fer-
ri, which is mine, and the one I select, as you
o generously offered, remains your own."

Rita frowned, unsurprised that he would hold
er to the offer of his choice from her selection,
ven after he had raised her offer to this more
udacious deal himself.

"I must continue my work," she said, the out-
ome of the entire agreement hinging on this
ne point.

She had not let her future husband and in-
aws, nor her own father, bar her from pursu-

ing her calling, and she would not let the Prin
do so, either.

He nodded without hesitation. "Of cours
Your work is the thing that makes any of th
make sense. You will have your own garage
Hayat, preferably equipped to your most extrav
gant and expensive whim and delight."

He didn't have to know her well to know th
he offered her the kind of thing that only a ve
few men in the world could—and that she wou
have a hard time resisting.

Her kind of garage didn't come cheap.

But he doesn't know you, a cautionary intern
voice reiterated.

But for the first sixteen years of her life, sh
had known that there was a great possibility tha
her husband would not know her until their wec
ding day, as had been the case for her own pa
ents.

The Prince might be a stranger, but unlike th
marriage she had thought she was going to hav
back then, beyond residence and legal status
he was not asking her to make any significan
changes to her life or person.

And while romance might not be on the table
what *was*, was a marriage that did not expec
her to sacrifice herself to anything but a tepic
dynamic.

That was certainly more appealing than fa-
miliarity or love.

In Rita's experience, love demanded too much—was conditional and controlling. Love clipped the wings and drained the batteries, using the heart to trap and coerce. Love left no room for creativity or innovation or freedom.

Instead of intimacy with an overbearing known, she could marry a stranger and continue her life of celibacy and fulfilling work alongside. She could marry a man who was content to let her remain entirely as she was right now.

"In sum," the Prince concluded his offer, his voice as convincing as any shaitan's, "if you agree to be my bride, you remain free to continue your work, your body remains your own, and you retain all but the agreed-upon vehicles in your fleet. And, following a few lavish years abroad, your life will once again be your own. Only you will have gained invaluable contacts and an incredible story to tell."

When she had been given the choice as a young woman between the cold comfort of trying to change the world and the warmth and love and devotion of starting her own family, Rita had chosen the former.

Now she was faced with a similar choice: a cold marriage that came with a real shot at changing the world, or staying right where she was as NECTAR, chipping away at her dream alone, one commission at a time.

Licking her lips, Rita drew in a deep bre
and said, "I'll do it."

Like a pair of Venuses in the night sky, triun
lit the prince's already-glowing eyes further st
His lips carried his mouth into a genuine, unce
trolled, smile—one that revealed bright, strai
teeth.

And then he laughed.

The sound was round and full and echoed
her garage, swirling around Rita like a fairy go
mother's magic, changing her irrevocably as
this were the beginning of an adventure and r
a marriage of strangers.

When his mini solar flare began to settle, h
eyes still glowing, his smile still wide, he sai
"To Rita, the motorhead princess." Raising an i
visible glass to her, he added, "I am certain th
this is the beginning of a beautiful arrangemen

Rita's stomach flipped at his words, her hea
fluttering at the same time.

It was the beginning of something, she knew
She just wasn't sure she'd use the word *beautifi*

Maybe impeccable... a sly voice teased in h
mind, but she tamped it down.

The Prince had been clear, and she had agree
theirs wasn't that kind of arrangement.

For her, it was about the dream that she ha
formed at her father's knee, a dream she wa
going to make come true, whether he was aroun
to witness it or not.

Across from her, the Prince stood, his form simultaneously still and thrumming, activating every area of her being—her imagination, her appreciation for beauty, her determination, her humor, her acknowledgment of fantastic design, her curiosity and even her body.

Though that isn't what this is about, she reminded herself.

Had she ever met a man who made machines seem primitive and weak in comparison to before?

She didn't think so. Humans were lopsided and prone to imperfection, but he was symmetrical, beautiful and strong.

Even her father had seemed small beside their family's fleet of big rigs.

She couldn't think of anything here the man who was going to be her husband would seem small beside.

With his car and his exhibition, and access to the world stage as a gorgeous prince's pretend wife, the Prince had just handed Rita a very real opportunity to change the way the world drove— far more of one than she had ever even had as NECTAR, boutique auto engineer for the globe's rich and famous.

Reaching into the pocket of her jumpsuit, she dug out her phone and dialed a number.

When she looked back up, the Prince had a

slight furrow to his brow, as if he had not like
the fact that she had escaped his gaze.

He would have to just learn to deal with tha
kind of frustration, though, because, as per thei
agreement, there were a lot of things she woul
be keeping to herself.

Her thoughts, for example.

He might be her fiancé, but they were stil
strangers, after all.

Infusing her voice with the cheerful distance
she used for client phone calls, Rita offered, "
don't know what your transport plan was for the
Ferrari, but I'm happy to arrange to include her
in my barge."

She could hire services to transport the irre-
placeable items she would need from her garages,
as well as to prepare the rest of her small compound—built with the money she'd earned as
NECTAR—for a long absence.

Retaining the groundskeepers on their regular maintenance schedules would ensure that the
landscaping retained its private oasis-like charm
while she was gone, as well.

Her cars, however, she would coordinate the
care and transport of herself.

"Barge?" the Prince questioned, breaking
into her preparations with a faint trace of distaste darkening his remarkable face. "You need
to bring so much that you have to coordinate a

arge? There is nothing you have here that I can-
ot replace to your liking in Hayat."

Looking at him as if he'd made the most lu-
icrous statement in the world, *because he had*,
Rita lifted an eyebrow and said, "Except for my
ars."

As if he had temporarily forgotten about her
private fleet and only now remembered, the
Prince's face lit with delight.

If he were truly a boy, rather than a man whose
dominating presence had just had a devastat-
ng effect on her five-year plan, he might have
clapped and jumped for joy at the reminder of
her fleet.

The man she was now engaged to might be
stranger, but he had a passion for cars, and that
was something.

Great love stories had been kindled out of less.

Not that theirs was a love story.

CHAPTER THREE

JAG HAD COME to get his car, and along the way he had picked up a wife.

What an unexpected development that had been.

He had already anticipated reaching his desired level of popular support within Hayat following his successful world exhibition, but with the added bonus of announcing his marriage, there would be no doubt.

And he had thought the trip to the United States was going to be a waste of precious time when he was so close to achieving his ends.

He was serious about his takeover being non-hostile. His people deserved peace, and he would do nothing to shatter that for them.

And he would secure that peace by first securing their love.

After all, there was no stronger force to compel human behavior, he knew, than love. In fact, he knew it better than most.

It was another reason why his little jaunt had

ved so fruitful. In Rita, he had found a woman
n whom he would never worry about manipu-
ng with emotions.

Rita was a virtual stranger, and by not allow-
them the space to become close there would
no emotional coercion and no accidental
rs—as his three friends had stumbled into in
fulfillment of their vows.

f love itself was powerfully coercive, then
ldren were its most effective tool.

People were willing to do anything for their
ldren—even die.

Jag was fond of free will.

Which did not mean he looked down on his
ends.

On the contrary, he was happy for them. In
eir cases, love had crept past their defenses and
riched their lives, the lovers they'd found trust-
orthy in their commitment to not manipulate.
The children they had produced were bless-
gs.

In fact, reflecting on it now, Jag oddly pre-
rred to see his friends happy and settled with
rong women and joyful families than where he
t, unexpectedly tied to a brilliant and beautiful
ut unwitting accomplice, that many steps closer
 achieving his ruthless goal.

But if his goal was ruthless and methods reso-
ate, it was at least to the benefit of the people he
uled and the woman he had joined himself to.

Following his proposal, his legal team had c ordinated expedited US licenses, documents a a local judge, who had arrived at the NECTA compound with the required paperwork and w nesses within the hour.

The ceremony had taken place in Rita's g rage, surrounded by the cars she had engineere and perhaps because of it, it was an experienc that Jag found more personal and unique tha any wedding he'd ever attended. Of course, th feeling could have come from the fact that it w; his own.

Like everything else about their meeting, was completely unlike any context within whic he had ever imagined getting married—and as prince there had been many of those—and yet i had been sentimental at the same time.

And funny.

In all of the rush of preparing for their hast marriage and immediate departure, Rita had no changed from her jumpsuit.

She had been married in NECTAR lime green his new wife, the world-famous genius mechanic

And when she first laid eyes on the private plane that now belonged to her as well, and which was just one of many, he heard her gasp even on the gusty tarmac.

It was rather adorable.

"Nice plane," she said breathlessly, gazing

ound the interior with adoration in her eyes as
ey boarded.

An unexpected surge of pride and pleasure
having decided to take the Cessna coursed
rough him as if it had always been his inten-
on to impress her when, in truth, he had sim-
ly wanted something that was both comfortable
nd fast.

He could have flown in his G6 but had chosen
peed over power for his unplanned excursion,
nd it made all the difference.

Seeing her enthusiasm, now he was glad he
ad for other reasons.

There was something cozy about the sweet
ittle jet with its designer interior.

Of all his jets, this was the most intimate and
omfortable and close, and sliding into the sup-
le comfort of the branded leather reclining seat
across from her, he appreciated that the small jet
created an atmosphere of intimacy around their
ake arrangement that he could not.

Was it fair that he had corralled this beautiful
and brilliant woman into a such a cold and trans-
actional marriage?

If she had not been so desperate to enter into
their deal for her own reasons, the answer would
likely have been no. But for whatever reasons—
and he knew it was more than the need to ensure
her work showcased well—she was.

"Why do you want to attend the exhibition

so badly?" he asked, interested in the backst
now that they were on their way back to Hay

To his surprise, his question brought a r
blush to his wife's cheeks.

"I told you. No one else can take care of
Ferrari but me. She's perfection on wheels,
with a race and the eyes of world leaders
around, she'll need maintenance. This isn't yo
everyday showcase."

She laid it all out very matter-of-factly, as
it were a completely reasonable justification
agreeing to marry a stranger and hare off ir
unknown waters.

Yet again, he could only admire her bald a
dacity.

The woman was completely undaunted.

She was also lying.

"What's the real reason, though?" he asked
a voice that brooked no denial.

Perhaps unsurprisingly, she denied it anywa
"That *is* the real reason. My name is on the line

"It's bigger than that," he insisted. "It has
be."

If he had not been surprised by her continue
denial, he *was* taken aback when her resistanc
crumbled.

"It's dumb," she muttered in a low voice.

"It's obviously not 'dumb' to you," he pointe
out. "In fact, I would hazard a guess that it ha
to do with something you care about very much

"I want to change the way the world drives," he whispered, almost under her breath, as if she were afraid to say it out loud to another person.

A number of feelings set off within him in reaction to her reluctant confession.

An unwarranted surge of protectiveness, the urge to fight and crush any force that threatened her fragile confidence and dream.

As idealistic as the words sounded, her decision made more sense now. Like every American he'd ever met, she wanted to save the world, and she was serious about it.

And, unexpectedly, he admired that dream and her dedication to it.

She had agreed to his terms not simply because she wanted to further her career as NECTAR, as he had assumed, but because she was truly committed to a better future, no matter how large a sacrifice it asked of her.

It was noble.

Because of that, he wasn't cynical when he responded. "If there is anywhere you can make an impact, it will be at this exhibition. You will have the attention of the world for however long it holds. There will be no better time to make a statement that will align it to your way of thinking."

Blush growing, her eyes glistened beneath the plane's lights, and he found himself caught in their wells.

Had she sparkled like she did now in the g rage? he wondered. *Or was it simply a trick their current lighting?*

Clearing her throat, she broke their stare a looked around, swallowing as she did so. Spea ing only after another beat of settling herse "The CJ has it all," she said finally, continuin "She can go far, she's comfy and cute, and sl has a pair of wings that were made to fly. If ever get the chance to try my hand at a plane, I start with a CJ."

Unable to help himself—and why should h even try when he was wealthy and powerful an could not give much beyond trinkets and platforn to a woman who wanted to save the world?—Ja indulged her.

"You can start with this one," he said, smilin at the delight that swept across her beautiful face

"Don't tease," she said cautiously. "If you don' mean it, don't say it."

He appreciated the casual way she ordered hin around. No one else had ever done that with him not even his friends.

"Why would I joke?" he said with a shrug. "I you mess it up, it's my oldest and smallest plane. I'll just get a new one."

Snorting, her smile still wide, she mocked him. *"I'll just get a new one."*

Grinning, he sighed, "Airplanes. They just don't seem to make them like they used to anymore."

"I can guarantee that no one will make one ⟨li⟩ke the one I make," she said, full of herself, ⟨an⟩d seeing the confidence on her made his grin ⟨str⟩etch wider.

She had earned every ounce of cockiness she ⟨po⟩ssessed.

Like her, the vehicle that she had built for him ⟨su⟩rpassed every one of his impossible standards.

Her work, her mind and her body were all ex⟨c⟩eptional.

All of that aside, however, they still needed ⟨to⟩ get their stories straight before they touched ⟨d⟩own in Hayat.

A frown coming to his brow along with the ⟨th⟩ought, Jag leaned forward in his seat.

"You've reminded me that even for an engi⟨n⟩eering genius there are still matters we should ⟨d⟩iscuss before arriving in Hayat."

Teasing at his new seriousness, Rita leaned ⟨f⟩orward, bringing her elbows to her knees, her ⟨e⟩yes direct on Jag's, and said, "Lay it on me, ⟨P⟩rince Jahangir."

Across the aisle from her, Jag grimaced. "Save ⟨m⟩e from Americans…" he muttered to himself, ⟨b⟩efore he said, "Well, for starters, you will not be calling me Jahangir."

The name left a bad taste in his throat every ⟨t⟩ime he said it, each syllable a reminder that his father saw him not as a human being, but as a prized possession. His name had been a reward

to a favored lackey, evidence from before he wa
even born that to his father, Jag's entire life wa
nothing more than an accessory to his power.

Rita frowned. "What should I call you then?"
she asked.

"My friends call me Jag," he said gruffly.

A slow smile spread across her face, mischie
lighting her eyes as she asked, "Does that mean
we're friends now?"

Snorting, he said, "Absolutely not. We're married. Friends is the last thing we are."

Smile not budging an inch, she slyly retorted,
"Whatever you say… *Jag*…" emphasizing and
lengthening his short moniker.

Or at least that's what it sounded like to him,
though in reality, it was probably only her teasing and forward nature unable to resist an opportunity to needle.

He may not know his wife well yet, but he had
become quite familiar with those elements of her
personality in the time they'd known each other.

Regardless of intent, however, he liked the
sound of it more than he probably should have.

He would need to be careful around the woman
he had just married.

She was forbidden territory, and recalling that
he really did have serious things he wanted to
go over with her, he attempted to steer the conversation back to them and far from the threat
her open and easy nature presented. "Now that

've settled that, we can move on to more im-
rtant things."

Clearly starting to enjoy herself, Rita leaned
even closer. "Is there really anything more im-
rtant than what I should call you? Maybe your
thday?" She tapped her finger to her chin in
ught.

"October twenty-ninth," he snapped, continu-
g, "I will have a dossier drawn up for you with
rtinent biological and preferential details later."

"Ooh, a dossier," she said, mocking his stiff-
ss and formality in a way that he refused to
ile at.

There were serious matters to discuss. Hold-
g back his grin with effort, he said, "While we
ill have some time before the public finds out
out you, and while I have been assured that my
eople will adore any bride I bring to them, we
ill must have a story to tell them. Obviously,
e will limit and minimize your public role as
rown Princess for the tenure of our agreement.
ou're quite occupied with your work, I'm sure,
nd there is no need to get the people attached to
temporary figurehead. While our ruse serves
any purposes, I am committed to ensuring that
does not negatively impact the people of Hayat.
n fact, beyond providing them with something
un to write about in the tabloids, this arrangement should not affect them."

"Admirable," Rita said sarcastically.

"What?" he asked, giving her a look. He on
raised normal considerations for a monarch.

"Nothing. Go on." She gave him a "carry o
gesture with her hand that he had the most i
fantile urge to ignore simply on principle, *and*
would have, had the continuation of their conve
sation not been necessary.

It was too bad she would not be serving in tl
capacity of a real princess, however, because h
little wave had been filled with enough royal co
descension to make a queen proud.

"As I was saying," he went on, nonethele
dogged by the strange sense that she had som
how outmaneuvered him, "we'll need an ente
taining and believable story to explain how a
American mechanic, albeit a world-famous on
snagged the Crown Prince of Hayat."

"That's funny, I remember it the other wa
around, with the Crown Prince of Hayat snag
ging the American mechanic," she said flatly.

"Regardless of how it happened, we need
unified story to tell."

"Forgive me for suggesting that it might b
best to stick as close to the truth as possible," sh
said, the sarcasm in her voice slipping a notcl
closer to irritation.

"You think people are going to believe that?'
he asked, lifting a brow as his urge to settle the
matter shifted more into one to egg her on further.

His new wife had a sparky temper, as he'd seen

the garage and throughout their acquaintance, d he found he liked the jolt of touching it.

And unlike most of the people he knew, Rita ever seemed reticent about sharing that part of erself with him.

It was refreshing to be in the company of meone unafraid to put him in his place the ay only his friends seemed to.

Not that his new wife was his friend.

Rita was merely his business partner, which e would just have to keep on reminding himself nce it was dangerously easy to forget while in onversation with her.

Wisely, she said, "I think people will believe hatever they want to believe, regardless of what le official story is."

"So cynical, Rita," he said, tsking at her with disapproving shake of his head before continu-1g, "And now you're confusing me. One minute ou want us to tell the truth that our alliance is eally just a strange political move, and the next ou want us to make up a story that's worth be-ieving?" Though it might have been rusty, his omedic tone achieved what he had been going or, and the stiffness in her posture and expres-ion broke with an exasperated smile.

"No, no," she grumbled, hands up in surrender is she deflated. "The people want good tabloids, o we will give them good tabloids," she added.

He didn't expect the strange surge of approval

that coursed through him at her words, a m[...]
placed sense of pride rising in him to have fou[...]
a woman who, like him, was willing to put [...]
needs of the people of Hayat before her own.

That, he believed, was the single most imp[...]
tant trait of a good ruler.

Ruling together, however, was not a part [...]
their deal.

And keeping that in mind was already sho[...]
ing itself to be slightly more complicated than [...]
had initially anticipated.

Once they landed in Hayat, he would endea[...]
to restrict the amount of time he spent in h[...]
presence.

It was perhaps unsurprising, but her combin[...]
tion of brilliant mind and royal irreverence ma[...]
it far too easy to relax his guard around her. I[...]
excused his lack of foresight with the fact that [...]
was an experience he hadn't often had.

"So, *Jag*, what kind of story do you propose[...]
she asked, doing that thing where she made h[...]
name sound like honey on her tongue again.

Once the wave of caress-like tingling stoppe[...]
coursing across his skin, Jag reflected that it ha[...]
perhaps not been his brightest idea to give h[...]
his casual name.

"Like-minded tech-loving young lovers' path[...]
cross over one-of-kind commission and spark[...]
fly?" he suggested flirtatiously, as if he'd m[...]
mentarily lost his mind.

The deep wells of her eyes locked on his, and she licked her lips before replying, "Better, Prince falls for mysterious engineer known the world over only as NECTAR."

A slow grin lifting the corners of his mouth in a way he knew that women loved, Jag's eyes lit with dare. "My version is closer to the truth."

Rita's breath quickened. "Mine is a better story."

"Says who?" he asked, his eyes never leaving hers.

"It's got mystery and romance, enough of both to keep people occupied filling in the details themselves."

"And just how did you become such an expert at subterfuge, I wonder, Rita," he murmured, eyes never leaving hers.

Rita waited a beat, swallowing and clearing her throat before replying, "Just the past six years of becoming one of the most famous conversion specialists in the world all while no one knew my name, face or gender."

"Strong points, dear wife. So why did we marry, then? Why not simply become famous lovers? Princes do it all the time," he teased, pushing her because the effect when he did— the way she got all strong and firm before his eyes, refusing to back down or be intimidated— set off thrills in his blood.

And she did not disappoint him now.

Tossing her head, throwing that thick, gloss
hair of hers over her shoulder in the process, sh
angled her chin up. "That was never on the tabl
prince or not. The mysterious mechanic migh
work on the cutting edge of technology, but sh
is still an old-fashioned Muslim girl from an old
fashioned Muslim and South Asian family."

Jag could not stop his eyes from flaring witl
the triumph at yet another welcome, if utterly unexpected, development. "Is that true, Rita? Abou
you, I mean? Are you a Muslim?" he asked.

Guardedness creeping into her eyes, Rita nodded, her answer a tentative, "Yes."

"Unbelievable," he uttered on an exhale, and
she frowned.

"What?" she asked warily.

"I just couldn't have planned it better myself.
Unsuitable, and yet infinitely suitable."

"What do you mean?" she asked, eyes narrowing with suspicion.

"You being a Muslim woman, I did not expect
it, but am beyond pleased."

"Why?" she asked.

"As a Muslim woman, you have removed
my father's greatest potential argument against
our marriage. I was prepared and, according to
national polls, Hayat was prepared for its first
non-Muslim princess, but now that is irrelevant.
When I debut you to the world as my bride, my

ather will have no excuse with which to invali-
ate our marriage."

"Your father would do that?" Rita asked, less
ghast than he might have anticipated coming
rom an American.

"I warned you that he was a ruthless tyrant. He
elieves it is a king's right to dictate the lives of
ll of those he encounters. As you might surmise,
have been less than amenable to those beliefs.
A great deal of your appeal as my wife lies in
your being the antithesis of what he would want
in a daughter-in-law, but while I am happy to
take every shot I can at my father, I never like to
do so at the expense of my people. The fact that
you are Muslim, however, will make it easier for
them. He will not be able to use religion to stir
up the wrong kind of controversy, and they will
find you more relatable."

"And here I'd always thought faith was a personal thing," she said dryly.

Jag laughed. "Nothing is personal when you
are royal."

"Yippee," she responded darkly, and Jag could
not hold back his laughter.

"Relax," he said, still quietly laughing. "You
are exactly the woman for the job. Our marriage
is expressly for the purpose of securing the approval of my people, and I would never bring
them a bride who I did not think would serve
them. The wrong woman in the position could be

disastrous, no matter how temporary the arrangement might be. But you, you just keep proving yourself more and more suited to the role. You're nothing my father would want for my wife, and yet everything my country is clamoring for. Announcing to the world that I have made NECTAR, the world's greatest electric conversion engineer, my bride as the grand finale of my international electric energies exhibition will not only be the coup d'état of my exhibition, but has the potential to be the kind of story that captures the attention of the world."

It was all so close, he could almost taste it.

CHAPTER FOUR

USUAL WITH her conversations with Jag, Rita's
nd zeroed in on the minutiae of what he said
ile sailing over the probably more important
rts.

"Debuting NECTAR?" she asked, fingers and
mbs suddenly and inexplicably numb.

Jag smiled, the visions of the future in his
es much clearer than what was before him.
f course," he said. "The future Queen of Hayat
ing the world's foremost expert on electric en-
nes and systems will catapult my vision into
ality far more efficiently than even the world's
rest car."

"No one in the world knows who NECTAR
," Rita said, as if stating the well-known fact
as evidence enough of the point she was try-
g to make.

"And because of that, the reveal will be that
uch more a sensation."

"I've kept my identity a secret for a reason."
any reasons, in fact, not the least of which in-

cluded not having to wade through the nonsen
of men who didn't respect women and being ab
to get away with charging what she did for h
work. She was the best there was at what she di
but there was just no way her clients would pa
a woman that much money for a job. Especial
when she had first started.

And then there was the fact that she hadn
wanted to cause her family to lose any more fac
There was no need to flaunt her disobedience–
to either of the families involved.

Jag shrugged insouciantly and waved the cor
cern away. "I'm sure it was a good one," he saic
"Circumstances now call for a change."

"It is easier to do my job when people thin
they are dealing with a man," Rita tried again.

Leaning forward, he took her hand, his ambe
gaze trapping hers. With deepest conviction h
said, "Imagine how easy it will be once the
know you are a princess."

Rita blinked, for a moment stunned by imag
ining it. Jag was right.

Princess.

She could probably charge even more.

But at the expense of the world knowing who
she was.

It was part of the deal—he had mentioned it
multiple times, in fact; she had just somehow not
put two and two together.

"We can't be more...*discreet* about that?" she asked, already knowing the answer.

Seriousness coming to his stare, Jag gave the slightest of head shakes. "Absolutely not, Rita. Not for what I'm about to do, and certainly not for what you want to do. You just said you wanted to change the world. That's not the kind of thing you do discreetly. This is your chance to jostle your place to the center of the world stage and sing as loud and strong as you can. People must know and love you if you have any hope of getting them to do what you say."

"You don't think it's a little overrated? People? I mean, look at all I've accomplished so far with just the help of a few people along the way," she said, gesturing around the cabin.

"You said you wanted to change the way the world drove, Rita. You don't achieve that by taking the driver seat in every car."

Again, he was right, though she only ceded the point with a nod.

She didn't think she liked it when he was right, the idea triggering a memory of her mother saying the same thing about her father.

She had thought of her parents more in her short time with her new husband than she had in years.

But it made sense that they would be on her mind on the day she got married. Her getting married had been what set everything off, after all.

Just like everything Jag was saying to
made sense. She had been willing to sign up
a facade of a marriage for the sake of this go
She would not let it be for nothing simply
cause she didn't want to stand in the spotli
and speak.

And why, in all that was good and beautif
did her mind keep coming back around to se

She knew it had to be because they had
pressly established that they would not be havi
sex, but even in defiance it was out of charact

She never thought about sex. Her mother h
drilled it into her that sex was a part of marria
and when marriage had been taken off the tal
for her, so too had sex.

And while others might have taken bei
shunned as freedom and permission to aband
the edicts and values that had been imposed up
them for the first eighteen years of life, Rita h
not. Instead, she had clung to them as the on
proof that she had ever had a family at all.

The fact that her family had been right—th
she'd only ever been interested in cars—made
easier. It was easy to walk what was left of th
line when she only noticed steel frames attache
to wheels.

Rita wasn't sure now if it was because she
already started down the slippery slope of forg
ing her morals and ethics by marrying him,
if it was just that she found herself sitting in th

ky under the spell of some kind of stunning and
wicked djinni, but for some reason, that wasn't
he case with Jag.

She was honestly having a hard time *not* no-
ticing Jag.

They had made the right choice in committing
to a marriage without physical intimacy. She was
sure of it, even as areas of her mind and body
were apparently in the process of waking from
their twenty-seven-year slumber.

She did not care about sex, even with Jag—
especially with Jag.

In fact, she hardly thought about either the opposite or same sex throughout the whole of her
existence.

It had been one of the greater divides between
herself and her peers all the way through school.

While early childhood friendships had flour-
ished in the playground context of racing and
chasing, as she had aged alongside other girls,
her attention had remained fixed upon the interests that had driven her childhood explorations,
while her peers became more and more interested
in, well, each other.

Like all of her idiosyncrasies, Rita had assumed the difference was just part of how she
was uniquely engineered. Her disinterest, in addition to the headscarf she had worn during that
era of her life, had not exactly prevented her from
making close friends, but certainly didn't help

her find common ground with anyone her ag
Being the only *hijabi* at her school often mea
that curiosity got in the way of friendliness, a
none of her classmates liked cars the way she di

But it hadn't mattered to her.

Her parents' opinions had been the only on
that mattered to her back then.

And after that, she had been matched and i
school and occasionally meeting her intended fo
chaperoned outings, and then after that, all she
had left were cars.

No marriage, no sex, and there hadn't bee
time for it anyway—not when she had been o
her way to becoming NECTAR.

Spending time in the presence of the stun
ningly and unconsciously sensual Crown Princ
of Hayat, however, was doing things to her sys
tem that she had never before experienced—un
comfortably activating processes that she had
been certain she lacked and sparking question:
and curiosities she had never felt.

And here on the plane with Jag made for neither a good time and place, nor partner, to be setting anything like this ablaze.

CHAPTER FIVE

As the jet descended into Hayat, having stopped
nce midway through the journey to refuel, Jag
ook in his homeland. It took him a beat longer,
though, to recognize the unfamiliar apprehen-
ion he felt as caring about what another person
thought. Did the woman who was his wife see
an expanse of large flat inkblot-black seas broken by stretches of abysmal beige—as he'd once
overheard a Westerner describe it—or did she
see the turquoise-azure sea meeting the ivory-
cream ocean of sand, pulsing and mixing at the
point of contact like freshwater meeting salt, as
he did?

As they neared the ground and Hayat City
proper, did she note the incredible and whimsi-
cal shapes of the great sand works that seemed to
float like lotuses at the top of the churning sea?
Did she see the incredible architecture, how the
traditional and ancient met the bold and new, the
oldest of humanity's histories jumping right into

the scientific and technological future of their collective imagination?

Did it matter?

Appreciating the beauty of the country she was the pretend Princess of wasn't why he'd married her. She was here to serve a different purpose.

It was absolutely irrelevant what she thought of Hayat or its capital.

But that did not stop him from feeling a sense of pride when she gasped as they touched ground and she got a good look at the city around her.

"I never realized... Would you look at the size... Is that a mosque?" Each statement was more like exclamations, most left incomplete, abandoned in favor of the next.

The flow of her words didn't stop, all the way through the airport and into the car that awaited them.

If he had wondered what she thought of Hayat, her enthusiasm gave him a strong suggestion as to the answer.

"And you're telling me that three of the world's ten tallest buildings are located here in Hayat?"

At his nod, she made yet another note in her phone. "We'll have to see all three."

She had begun taking notes as soon as their driver entered traffic and they passed two parked police vehicles.

"That was an Aston Martin One-77 and a

kan Hypersport!" she had squealed joyously. or the police!"

Since then, she'd hardly stopped jotting things wn.

Observing her, he sent a text to the head of his am to coordinate a new encrypted device for r use. Her US-based carrier and model would too easy to break into here in Hayat.

And, while his mind was on the topic of pre- ring her for Hayat, he needed to do something out her clothing.

As was the case in Dubai, Hayat City's citizens ided themselves on living on the front lines of shion, with straight-from-the-runway couture common sight on the streets.

Her wide-legged American blue jeans, baggy veatshirt and canvas sneakers would not do.

Beyond that, the getup was inappropriate ecause it was far too warm to wear in Hayat ity—even for the purpose of strolling from a imate-controlled car into a climate-controlled uilding interior.

Retrieving his phone from his pocket, he called is secretary, catching Rita's attention in the pro- ess. "Alert my tailor that we are on the way and ill be using the private entrance."

Rita had paused her back-seat tourism and was oking at him quizzically.

"We need to outfit you like a princess," he xplained.

She looked down at her clothes, then back
at him. "I thought we were waiting to announ
until the race. I was really hoping to see the st
dium first."

And to push the debut from your thoughts. F
noted her lingering reticence on that point, b
said only, "There will inevitably be photos of u
taken before then. The moment we leave this v
hicle, our game is on. There is no room for mi
step. You must look the part even while playin
the mysterious stranger at my side."

She narrowed her eyes at his words, pressin
her lips into a line, but ultimately shrugged an
returned to taking in the city as they travele
through it, and he found himself curious as t
what she was thinking.

The driver made the turn into the belowgroun
entrance of the secured building, and Jag smile

Their wardrobe problem would soon be a thin;
of the past.

Rather than a standard elevator, the drive
guided their car into a vehicle elevator.

Visitors to residents of the tower drove righ
into the elevator with an access code and wer
lifted, in situ, to the private floors of the individ
ual they were calling on. The majority of resi
dents had selected the floor plan that included the
facade of indoor/outdoor living, which allowe
their visitors to exit the elevator into the facade
of a residential street front.

Jag's chauffeur parked faux-street side and came round to open the doors for both Jag and Rita.

Stepping out, Rita was agog. "We're inside a building still, right?" she asked, looking around at the shockingly realistic outdoor residential street scene.

The "sky" above them was intelligent, programmable according to the owner's weather and daylight preferences. Currently, a balmy blue sky shone above while an artificial warm breeze swirled a floral scent around them.

Jag nodded, smiling at the note of awe in her voice. "We are."

Rita's eyes sparkled as she took it all in, the glowing wonder in them stopping here and there to peruse the hidden joints that held up the mirage.

She examined the one-way windows, which let light stream in for the "outdoor" plants without interfering with the artificial climate.

"How extraordinary," she breathed, sounding more like a scientist at the moment of eureka than a garage denizen.

As NECTAR, perhaps the mad scientist label was more accurate.

She should not have looked the part in the least, this woman dressed like an American teenager, but she did.

She had the kind of wild genius that had a hard time hiding itself.

Despite clothing being the reason they had entered the luxury building, Jag could not help note that, more so for her than anyone else he ever met, clothes did not make Rita.

Nothing she wore, it seemed, had the capac to hide her bright intelligence, nor her beauty, the way her eyes constantly darted around a analyzed—not a lime-green jumpsuit, and no sweatshirt and old trainers.

In every setting and costume, the woman w stunning.

But just because form could not hide her fun tion, it did not mean that her form could not enhanced.

And as if the conclusion conjured him, Jag tailor chose that moment to open his front doc

"Prince Jahangir, your visit is as welcon as it is unexpected." The man's voice was lo and warm and, as always, modulated to conve friendship.

Jag was willing to tolerate a certain level theatrics in the pursuit of a perfect suit.

"Jameel, you are a paragon of style, as ever Jag said, smiling.

Jameel waved off the compliment. "I wear th same thing every day."

"There is no need to change when you ar leagues ahead of the rest."

"Flattery, Prince? You must have a dire need

Jag laughed before indicating Rita's presenc

with a nod of his head. "Not I. I bring you a challenge from America."

Jameel's gaze traveled from the Prince to Rita, who had returned to Jag's side from examining the mirage walls that were in truth one-way windows.

"Oh, dear," Jameel said, shoulders slumping as he took in the whole of Rita's person. "How much time do I have?" he asked, a slight wobble in the shield of confidence he typically exuded.

"For a complete wardrobe? A week. For something more appropriate for daywear in Hayat City? None. She cannot leave the premises like this."

Taking in a shuddering breath that concluded with an expression of resolution, Jameel nodded. "I don't have much here right now, but your timing is impeccable, as always, Prince. Your father's youngest wife recently commissioned a new set. I've a few pieces completed that I can make adjustments to." Eyeing Rita, Jameel began taking mental notes. "Let out the bust, bring in the waist, lengthen the pant, and we'll be set."

Bemused, Rita laughed. "Just all that?" Her voice was charming and melodic, bolstered by her curiosity and engaged mind, and even the jaded tailor looked momentarily mesmerized.

Jag could not have found a better partner in this endeavor.

However, he had brought her to Jameel not

to assess her capacity to make everyone sh
met fall in love with her. He'd brought her fo
some clothes.

Answering his wife in order to remind the tai
lor of their purpose in being here, Jag said, "Lik
in all design, impeccable attire comes down to
the details, my dear."

Directing his attention more fully on Rita, Ja
meel said, "You're rather beautiful, you know,'
as if he were surprised to only now realize it.

Brushing aside the strange spurt of possessive
aggression that rose within him upon noting the
other man's gaze, Jag agreed. "Indeed, she is a
diamond in the rough."

An odd expression flashed across Rita's face
at Jag's words, but she smiled at Jameel and said,
"Thank you."

"Who are you?" Jameel's question seemed to
slip free without his realizing that it was a mon-
umental breach of the discretion he was famous
for.

For his part, Jag understood.

There was something powerfully magnetic
about his new bride. Something about her ap-
proachable appeal frayed the seams of even the
strongest sense of propriety.

Because of that, and because there was no time
like the present to practice the winding naviga-
tion of their story, rather than ignoring Jameel's

uestion, Jag answered with a careful truth. "She
s NECTAR."

Jameel's mouth dropped open, and again Jag
was impressed by the uniqueness of the situation.

Jameel regularly outfitted the kings and queens
of the world—that he was moved to shock upon
meeting this particular woman spoke volumes.

"B-but… I had no idea NECTAR was a
woman…" Jameel stammered.

"I trust you'll have no problem outfitting a
woman."

"Certainly not," Jameel said absently, tossing
a "help yourself to the refreshments" over his
shoulder as he led Rita off.

Two hours later, Jag's diamond had been pol-
ished to a shine.

"Prince Jahangir, may I present the newest
NECTAR conversion to hit the world, the mad
genius herself?" Jameel's voice held the humor
of an inside joke, and Jag opened his eyes to another surge of possessive feeling.

He had not brought her to Jameel to develop
a rapport; he had brought her here for a casual
outfit for a princess.

But upon laying his eyes on her, thoughts of
jealousy fled Jag's mind.

A change of clothing should not have transformed the woman the way it had.

And to be fair it wasn't that she looked different, per se.

The same bright glowing brown face smiled at him, with the same big glossy eyes and the same lushly full lips.

Her heart-shaped face was the same, with the same charming pointed chin, with its faint hint of cleft, and the same perfect white teeth and the same straight brown brows and thick curling lashes, each feature emanating the same sheen of health and vibrancy that they had had before she'd gone away with the tailor.

It was only her clothing that had changed, but the difference was night and day.

Jameel had outfitted her in slim-cut ankle-skimming black pants whose thick black satin material retained a gentle structured form while at the same time flowing smoothly with the movements of her legs.

For her top, Jameel had chosen black as well, dressing her in a three-quarter-length-sleeve tunic with a mandarin collar and decorative clasps.

It was the astounding embroidered long coat, though, that truly made the look.

Technically a long sleeveless vest, the black garment was made to be worn open, falling to about knee-length and embroidered with what Jag knew would be real gold thread that had been woven into intricate and detailed geometric and star patterns along the front and lower edges of it.

The effect was natural and effervescent, bold

future-minded, while remaining respectful
radition. She looked exactly like the conver-
ns she created.

Once again, the clothier had proved himself to
of the highest order.

Jameel did not merely drape fashionable
thes on bodies. He used fashion to express
souls that the bodies contained.

Rita's accessories were gold and glittering—
hands and wrists and ears and neck draped
th copious amounts of diamonds and black
arl–accented rings, bracelets, necklaces and
rrings. Each piece caught the light in much the
me way as her skin tone did, catching and re
icting it back out into the world more joyously.

Jag swallowed, unsuccessfully attempting to
calibrate himself in the material world.

"Fortunately," Jameel said, midway through
plaining Rita's attire, which Jag only now re-
ized, "your stepmother had not yet seen my
oncepts or pieces so she will never know what
e missed out on."

"It was meant for Rita," Jag said.

"Without a doubt," Jameel added, his eyes
glow with his creation.

Jag looked to Rita, catching her gaze, unable to
ass up an opportunity to feel the strange bolt of
onnection that came every time their eyes met.
Her pupils dilated, distracting him from her

clothing as they pulled him deeper, lulling hi[m]
into following her lead.

The smile that blossomed on her face was wi[de]
and unguarded and sweet as anything that J[ag]
had ever seen, and he was transfixed. Until [he]
shook himself free with a frown.

As much as it might appear from the outset th[at]
they were here spoiling his new bride, that w[as]
not the case and he, above all apparently, neede[d]
to remember that.

"I'm never taking it off!" Rita exclaime[d,]
proud of how she looked despite the war goin[g]
on within him.

Her delight was fresh and nourishing like [a]
dip in the nectar she'd so aptly named herself fo[r,]
making him realize how starved for simple, hon[-]
est sweetness he had been all this time.

But not from her. He could find that sweetnes[s]
from any other source but her.

To remind them both of the distance they'[d]
agreed to, Jag nodded to break their connectio[n]
and cleared his throat, offering a stiff smile an[d]
a clipped, "Excellent."

Glancing between the two of them, Jamee[l]
laughed. "It was an honor to dress you, Rita. Yo[u]
have my number. Don't hesitate to call if you eve[r]
need anything."

Not liking the sound of that, Jag lifted his arm
to his wife. She crossed to him to take it without thought, brushing off Jameel's very serious

ffer as if he just gave his direct number out to
l of his clients.

Leading her back to the artificial street and
eir driver, Jag was glad to return to the ve-
icle elevator and once again capture her atten-
on. She had the confounding habit of finding
nything and everyone outside of him infinitely
ore fascinating than she seemed to find him,
nd he didn't like it.

"What did you think of Jameel?" he asked as
oon as they were comfortably situated within
he car.

"He cares about clothing the way I care about
ars and was full of advice about Hayat."

"Well said. And what advice did he give?"

"There is always someone watching."

"Again, he's correct. Fortunately, now you are
dressed for the audience."

She snorted, and he smiled, glad she had heard
he joke in what he had said and proud of her.

As far as dry runs went, their stop by the tai-
or's had been perfect.

Rita had charmed Jameel exactly as Jag predicted she would charm all of Hayat.

Now Jag just had to figure out how he felt
about it.

"Where are we going now?" she asked.

"The stadium," he replied, and was rewarded
by another megawatt smile. She was like a living
Edison bulb—almost too bright to look at directly.

At the stadium, the driver had barely open
the door before Rita launched herself out of
car, virtually running toward the construct
site. Only waving an American flag as she
could have better displayed to the world wh
she came from.

But her enthusiasm was rather pleasing. A
he was proud of the stadium.

Very near completion, it was the largest stru
ture in the world of its kind.

Catching up to Rita where she stood in t
shade of scaffolding, her palm placed flat agai
its surface, Jag asked, as if in all seriousnes
"What do you sense?"

Laughing, she pitched her voice into the real
of science fiction and horror, and crowed, "I
alive!"

Surprisingly, he caught himself smiling alon
side her though he was not typically one for su
silly jokes. His sense of humor and play was be
showcased in situations that he and Rita wou
not be finding themselves in.

Had agreed not to.

Attempting to pull his mind back from th
edges of what it was thinking, Jag defaulted
the dry and factual. "In truth, it *is* alive. Whe
completed, this building will be the largest bi
philic structure in the world."

At his side, Rita nodded in appreciation. "Ou
standing. I took a course on biophilic design ov

a summer semester once. It inspired a lot of the renovations I did in my home and garages. It's really the way of the future..." She trailed off as she explored the wall in closer detail, noting especially where the living elements joined with the artificial.

Jag watched her, oddly rapt, as she gently probed and felt the structure.

Her hands were quite small, he realized only now.

He had not noticed the fact while in her garage, nor during their plane journey, but now, as if every moment with her promised a new revelation.

How unexpected it was, that such small hands were solely responsible for creating some of the most advanced electric engine systems on the planet.

"You do renovations as well, now?" Jag asked, a single eyebrow lifted. "I didn't know I had conscripted a woman of all trades."

Rita turned to him with a smile and a laugh that knocked him back a bit, though she didn't seem to notice. "You do everything when you're just starting out and growing a business at the same time."

"And here I thought it was all about the cars for you."

Still easy and smiling, she returned to her exploration of the building as she answered, "It is, but as hard as it might be for a man like you imagine, there are a lot of roadblocks along the way to progress, and they're usually financial. Whenever I ran out of funds to pay for garage or home improvements, which happened pretty much between every commission at first, I was left with the choice of either scrounging up materials and figuring out how to do it myself or twiddling my thumbs and waiting."

Jag smiled, familiar enough with her by now to know she was not a woman who waited for things. "Impressive." He commended her with a nod.

Turning, she caught his eye and once again they shared a heartbeat of simply staring, before she remembered to smile and gave him a shrug. "It's just the way my family always operated."

"Well, it's made you well-versed. You should make something for my father," Jag said, trusting she had gleaned enough of the picture now to realize what an absurd idea that was.

She didn't let him down.

Chuckling, she said, "From what you've told me, I'm sure he'll love that. 'Here you go, Father-in-Law, even more evidence that your new princess is…dun-dun-dun…handy.'"

Laughter danced in Jag's eyes, even as mention of his father reminded him that until the announcement was made, it was still better to limit the amount of time Rita spent out and about.

magine his horror," he agreed, before adding,
As excited as you are, my dear, it is best I show
you your new home."

He hadn't meant to call her *my dear*, just as
he had not meant to allow his mind and body to
drift off into familiar and flirtatious behavior the
countless other times they had since he and his
bride had agreed to keep things professional between them, but it happened nonetheless.

After a good night's rest, and some time away
from his blushing bride, however, he would have
no problem maintaining the warm and unemo-
tional facade of a royal husband.

And in the meantime, he would take her to
his mother's old palace. With its custom design
and elaborate gardens it was the only one of his
palaces or residences that seemed remotely right
for the vibrant woman at his side, despite the fact
that he hadn't set foot inside it in years.

CHAPTER SIX

A WEEK LATER, Rita met Jag in the palace's central open-air courtyard beside its gorgeous centerpiece, a massive mosaicked fountain.

She hadn't intended to be there when he arrived.

She had simply finished the project she was working on too late to start a new one before dinner so had gone early to clean up in the palace baths and just happened to be crossing back at the same time that Jag entered from the hallway that led to the old garage.

She had only been in residence for a full week, and her new garages were nearly complete.

Smiling, her wet hair wrapped up in a towel and her body draped in the lovely linen pants and fitted cotton T-shirt that Jameel had made for her, Rita said, "Hi."

His answering smile was warm and sexy and a little surprised, and Rita had to tamp down the series of events that it set off in her body.

We might be husband and wife, she had to re-

nd herself, *but we both agreed that real in-
tiacy, emotional or otherwise, would only
mplicate things.*

She had not had to remind herself of the fact
a while—not since the Prince had settled her
before leaving the palace for wherever he re-
led the first night they arrived.

In fact, she had not seen him in person since
en.

They had spoken on the phone and exchanged
ultiple messages in the preceding week—about
r needs, and the construction of the new ga-
ges and discussions of how she might be incor-
orated into the exhibition at this late stage—but
e had not seen him.

*And it only took a few minutes for the wild
oughts to begin,* her inner critic noted tartly.
*ou need to get more serious about keeping
ings professional.*

"Hello to you," he said, a faint trace of breath-
ssness to his words. "You've been enjoying the
aths, I see."

Appreciating the opportunity the small talk
rovided to settle her system, Rita nodded.
They're wonderful. I can't believe I never
ought to do something like that back home."

"They were my mother's pride and joy. She
esigned them herself. It's been years since I've
sed them, though. I should."

"You absolutely should! It's a shame to think

they'd gone unused. It's the first thing I'm goin
to add when I return home. I bought my proj
erty because there was enough room for my g
rages and it was close to the city, but the hous
wasn't much when I got it. Nobody else wante
it because it's a heritage building and couldn't b
torn down, only renovated. It took me a while t
get to it since the garage had to come first, bi
as soon as I could, I refurbished it back to it
mid-century brilliance. I haven't touched the ol
pool yet, though. It doesn't even have any wate
in it—" She stopped herself when she realize
she was rambling on and gracelessly shifted sul
jects. "Your mother was a designer?" Rita askec
the question slipping out before she could thin
to stop it. Asking personal questions wasn't an
more of a good idea when they were trying t
keep things collegial between them than think
ing inappropriate thoughts.

But rather than withdraw further, her questior
seemed to relax his guard.

"She was," he said with a faint smile. "Interior
as well as an architect. She was rather brilliant
not unlike yourself," he added with a nod to Rita
"This palace was her doing, in fact."

Heat came to her cheeks at his words, the expe
rience of being praised by someone whose opin
ion mattered unfamiliar after so many years.

In fact, she couldn't recall it since the day
her father had announced the acceptance of her

atch when she was seventeen. Had it really been
n years?

"It's stunning," Rita said honestly. It really
as. In the week she had been here, Rita had
uly come to feel as if Jag's mother's palace was
home away from home, with its somehow warm
id comfortable elegance and class.

"I shared many happy memories with her
ere," he added, unprovoked.

As if the volunteered information were per-
iission to prod more, another question popped
ut. "What happened to her?" Rita asked, once
gain unable to keep her curiosity to herself, but
iis time it was not rewarded.

Rather, when he next spoke there was a thread
f distance in his voice that hadn't been there be-
ire, as if her question had brought him to his
enses and he'd closed entirely up, which was
robably for the best. At least one of them didn't
eem to be having trouble recalling the terms of
heir arrangement. "That's a sad story for another
ime," he said. "But I appreciate the reminder
bout the baths. A long soak in the large hot pool
vould no doubt do wonders for my shoulders."

Rita's mind's eye snagged on the image of Jag's
ong, muscular body stretched out in the largest
of the otherworldly baths. Chest strangely tight
ind breathless, she nodded, focusing on bring-
ng her system back under control rather than
ushing further.

She wasn't supposed to push. She was su-
posed to smile and retain professional distanc

Making another attempt at it, she said, "You
here in time for dinner. Will you be joining
She kept her voice light and airy for all that s
looked him in the eye, trying, if not entirely su
ceeding, at keeping things bland.

But it was a challenge, because in the we
that she had been living in the palace, this w
the first time she had seen Jag since he h;
dropped her off.

The corners of his mouth lifted ever so sligh
and he swallowed before nodding. "I canceled n
call with Sheik Ahmed. He will attend the exh
bition or he will not. I found I didn't care enou;
either way to miss Rafida's cooking in order
convince him."

"Is that so?" Rita asked, her breath oddly sh;
low and chesty.

It couldn't be just Rafida's cooking that h;
lured him back to the palace, though.

Rafida had confided to Rita that before Ri
arrived in Hayat, the Prince had rarely set fo
in the home of his childhood.

"I had a craving I could not resist," he said, ar
Rita would have sworn he was not talking abo
food, had he not been the one between them mo
firmly committed to the terms of their agree
ment. "I assume we're dining in the blue room'
Jag asked, shaking her from her thoughts as h

took a step back from her as if he only just now realized he stood too close, though she supposed that she, too, only now realized how near they had come to each other.

He had taken his suit jacket off as he spoke, having opted for Western attire for whatever business the day's agenda had included for him, and this time it was Rita's turn to swallow, nodding her response to save herself from having to clear her throat.

The blue room was one of her favorites in the palace.

A small formal dining room, it wasn't simply blue; that was merely the shorthand for it. In actuality, it was a gorgeously decorated room, graced with teal-trimmed wainscoting that was delicately overlaid with a faint gold leaf lattice pattern that seemed to shimmer and glow in both natural and artificial light, and floor-to-ceiling panel windows. Above the wainscoting, a stunning lagoon scene was painted across the walls, with cranes and weepy foliage all in lovely muted water tones.

Against the backdrop of the high-tech city, the room—the entire palace really—was a tranquil retreat, despite the fact that she hadn't explored Hayat City enough yet to need a retreat from it.

On the car ride from the racetrack to the palace, Rita and Jag had agreed that it was best for

her to keep a low profile, remaining for the mos
part in the palace, until after the exhibition.

That would keep the public's attention focuse
on the event while Rita's wardrobe was com
pleted. It also allowed her to push the whole ide
of debuting to the world to the back burner o
her mind.

Thus far, nothing this wild arrangement ha
asked of her had caused any permanent change
to the way she did business, but revealing to the
world that NECTAR was a woman undoubtedly
would.

If Jag was right, being a princess would offset
the loss of respect she would undoubtedly experience in the public eye once everyone knew she
was woman, but if he was wrong, it would take
a long time to recover.

And it wasn't like princesses exactly com-
manded respect in the auto industry—not to mention in engineering and computer science. They
were fields that, unfortunately, still just didn't
really take women seriously.

But she *would* be able to weather the storm
because she *would* be a princess.

At least temporarily.

And when she was no longer a princess, she
would have been openly operating as NECTAR,
the woman, for long enough that her work would
once again speak for itself.

She hoped.

"What's going on in that mad genius mind of ours?" Jag asked, breaking into her thoughts.

Starting, she had to pause in her steps for a moment.

Readjusting to the reality of company was a strange novelty. She had spent so much time alone that she wasn't used to someone pulling her back from her thoughts.

In fact, dinner tonight, with company, unexpected as it was, was something that had not happened in her life since she'd graduated from college.

After being disowned by her family nearly a decade ago, she had not been invited to any family gatherings, following the Friendsgivings of college. When her few friends had returned to their families of origin or begun starting families of their own, she'd felt like too much of an imposition to sit in.

In fact, far more than the physical intimacy they were committed to avoiding, sharing a meal together felt dangerously close and personal.

But that was probably just because she was used to the life of a hermit.

She was sure the Prince knew what he was doing.

Arriving in the dining room, they found that Rafida had set the table, but not yet laid it with food.

Jag sat at the north end of the table and Rita

took the seat to his left, it being the spot that made the most sense, conversation-wise.

She didn't want to have to yell at him across the table.

As they settled, Jag asked, "How did your work go today?"

Smiling, Rita said, "Good. The tools that have arrived so far are already making me realize how out-of-date my garage had become. I can't wait for the whole work space to be completed. It's so much more fun to work with top-of-the-line equipment," she said, pleasure rippling through her. "What about you? I mean besides the phone call you skipped."

Chuckling at her sass, Jag said, "Oh, I got a few things accomplished, one of which was approving the final schedule for the finale and NECTAR's, and my wife's, debut. It will take place at the race after-party. Where a highly selective guest list and a great deal of media will be in attendance. I anticipate announcing not just the triumph of the remarkable NECTAR Ferrari, but also the triumph of having won the infamous engineer's heart."

Once again there was a skip in the smooth flow of their conversation as Rita stilled upon hearing his words.

Of all the sacrifices she had been asked to make for her chance to change the world, the loss of her anonymity and the protective shell

the world thinking she were a man was the
most difficult.

It had not been easy to protect who she was,
and a part of her still wasn't convinced that giving it up was the best call.

When Rita waited too long to nod her enthusiasm or say something in response, Jag frowned
at her. "You're still nervous."

Seeing no point in denying it, Rita didn't. "I
am. Anonymity has been a security blanket for
me," she admitted. "It's hard to let it go."

"You're not a little girl, Rita, and you don't
have little-girl ambitions. I say that it's well past
time you let go of the blanket."

"Well, if you're going to put it like that," she
said, teasing to keep things light, but he wouldn't
let her.

"I am, because it is true. As I said on the plane,
you might have had your reasons and convic-
tions for keeping yourself a relative secret from
the world for this long, but you're going to have
to be brave enough to set them down if you want
to do the thing you said you want to do, that I believe you want to do. You wouldn't be here if you
didn't. Don't let self-doubt sabotage you now that
you're here. Unless you are ashamed of being a
woman," he added the last to his little speech as
if the idea had only just now occurred to him.

"Of course I'm not," Rita sputtered. "I'm extremely proud to be a woman, especially in my field."

"Your field? So it's being a mechanic, then?"

Rita snorted. "There's nothing else I've eve wanted to be. Absolutely nothing. But the fiel doesn't feel the same way about women in th ranks."

He waved her words away. "You've so fa surpassed the skill and reach of all of the goo old boys that that reality, unjust as it may be is no longer an excuse. If you're not afraid an ashamed, then I can see no reason why you woul hesitate to own who you are on the world stage Evolution is the constant process of releasing that which no longer serves you. Anonymity wa merely a tool to make your way to a place of rea power. Now that you've arrived at the threshold you can't let fear and old habits keep you from walking through the door."

Unable to think of anything to say to him, Rita smiled, knowing the expression was flat because she didn't particularly feel like smiling, and Jag frowned in response, but Rafida chose that moment to enter with their dinner service, saving her from having to say more on the subject.

The table was soon filled with platters of succulent seasoned and grilled meats and vegetables served over flavorful steaming rice, bowls of delicious slow-cooked porridges seasoned with freshly ground herbs and spices, and a large tray of fresh-baked flatbreads, as well as dishes overflowing with dates, homemade yogurt topped

ith honey and sesame seeds, fresh sliced fruit,
eep-fried dough balls liberally sweetened with
ate syrup, and a large, condensation-dripping
itcher of water infused with mint and honey.

How Rafida and her family managed to find
he time to care for and run Jag's large palace as
vell as do the cooking for three meals a day—as
he had been since Rita's arrival—was beyond
Rita's comprehension.

Of course, much to the dismay of her mother,
he greater bulk of domesticity was beyond Ri-
a's comprehension. It had been one of the things
hat had made negotiating a marriage arrangement for her initially difficult.

Sure, she was smart, but mothers wanted to
know their sons and grandchildren weren't going
to starve. It was just another one of the reasons
he offer from Rashad's family had been so
warmly received by Rita's.

They hadn't needed a girl who could cook, just
one who could become a doctor.

But Rita had just never been able to find the
same kind of passion for putting together a meal
or healing a wound as she had for building an engine, and it showed—even if she hadn't known
about the doctor part back then.

*It's love that makes the work fulfilling, du-
lali,*" her mother had assured her. "*I was just like
you as a young woman, never interested in the
housework or cooking. But then you and your sis-*

ter came, and it all changed. When you have ch *dren, you will see. You will want to feed them*

But children had not featured prominently her future visions then. And now they did even less.

Though her current business-arrangeme marriage was something different, normal a ranged matches were still common in her cor munity, even among American Bengalis.

Like Rita and Jag, her parents had only m for the first time on the day they were marrie but practices had changed since then.

When it was clear that Rita would be on successful and advanced track educationally, h parents were approached with match offers. Rea izing the time had come whether they were read or not, they officially began the process with th caveat that no marriage could take place befo. she had graduated from college.

The process was eventually settled with Ri engaged to a fellow Bengali-American youn man from a family of doctors.

Because Rita had been so young, still ju seventeen at the time, she and Rashad had bee granted six years to finish their undergradual educations and date and get to know each othe before they were to be married. And Rita woul go so far as to say she had become comfortabl with Rashad. He was smart and nonthreatenin and made easy small talk.

But then she had gone and unwittingly violated the terms of their arrangement, causing her family to lose face and her to be disowned. So here she was, instead, eating a delicious meal that she had not prepared in a business-arrangement marriage with a handsome prince and no prospect of change.

Which was exactly what she wanted.

In fact, her only regret was not realizing for so long that her parents' love and approval had hinged so strongly on that of her future in-laws.

That would have been nice to know way back in the beginning.

Fortunately, things with Jag had been spelled out from the start.

"You've gone quiet again," Jag noted, bringing her back into the present moment once more.

"Just enjoying the delicious meal," she lied, smiling and hoping he didn't look past her explanation.

Of course, taking in the fascinating lines and planes of the Prince, noting the curves of his lips and the barely restrained electric power in his gaze, it wasn't long before there were no more morose thoughts to hide.

"Rafida does not disappoint," he said.

Rita agreed. "She does not. She made the most delicious *balaleet* this morning," she said, grasping at the straw of chatting about food.

Jag made a noise of disappointment at the

news, and Rita was struck by the normalcy of
the moment.

It would be so easy to believe they were a normal husband and wife, when in truth, they were merely business partners.

"Rafida's *balaleet* is the best in the world. It was my mother's favorite," he said, a soft, unguarded smile on his face.

For the second time that night, he had brought up his mother. This time, she knew better than to push too hard.

"Really?" Rita said, forcing her voice to remain casual. "I hadn't realized Rafida had been in your service for so long."

"Rafida was my mother's housekeeper," he said.

"Really?" Rita exclaimed, genuinely taken aback. While Rafida was no spring chicken, neither did she seem old enough to have been with a family through multiple generations.

Laughing, Jag said, "She was very young when my mother hired her. Just fourteen."

"That is legitimately child labor," Rita noted.

Looking askance at her, Jag waved her words away. "Some rules are better broken until someone in a position of power can come along later and change them. Rafida was assaulted, and her family shunned her as a result. At the time, that was more common. Since I have stepped into my role as Crown Prince, things have changed."

"That's so awful for Rafida, though," Rita said, eart heavy.

Jag nodded. "My mother defied everyone, including my father, and gave her a good job. She ffered her education as well, but Rafida refused, nowing she would not be as welcomed at school s she was in my mother's home."

In a single anecdote, he had revealed the kind f woman his mother had been, far more than the etails he had mentioned earlier. And he had revealed how strong and resilient the woman Rita ad been sharing a home with was, as well.

Solemnly, Rita said, "Your mother sounds like generous and brave woman. And Rafida stronger than I even realized." Sensing without his indicating that he had once again gone as far as he vas willing, Rita then deliberately joked, "With wo powerful women as role models, it's too bad you turned out the way you did."

What her gibe lacked in sophistication—which was a lot—it made up for in efficacy.

Instead of the flare-up of flame in his copper eyes, of his walls going up again, the Prince moved.

As quick as a mongoose, his finger darted out to bop her nose.

Her eyes widened and her breath caught, her skin instantly sparking to life where he'd touched her, but he was unaware of the affect his contact was having on her.

Instead, his eyes triumphant but still some-how light and teasing, he said, "And what about you, Rita?"

"What about me?" she hedged.

"What about your family? Parents, siblings, all of it. Tell me about my in-laws." His questions were not requests but commands, given as if he'd only now just realized she might have a family history herself.

Likely, he only had.

Even without the need to defy him out of principle, family was a subject about which she didn't have much to share.

"My family," she repeated, buying herself time.

What should she start with? What could she tell him that would satisfy a mind that she knew would be looking for hints and details into her background without also revealing dark secrets and wounds that she did not know him well enough yet to discuss?

As curious as she was herself, she knew it was a delicate balance to satisfy someone while retaining your privacy, which was why as NEC-TAR she didn't even bother.

She lived in the mystery.

"My family owns a long-distance trucking company," she said. "My grandfather started it when he came to the United States with my grandmother as a young man and currently my ther and US-based uncles run things. I grew going on long-haul runs with my father every mmer." Rita paused, thinking of what to say ext. What she came up with would have to be ersonal enough to reveal a truth about herself ithout giving any hints as to how it all ended. ven years after it had all happened, she could ot shake the stings of guilt and shame, nor the ar that—in the end and in the eyes of anyone utside of the situation—her actions had not been inciploed and righteous, but selfish.

"My parents had an arranged marriage," she id. "My father flew to Bangladesh where he et my mother on the day of their wedding. They ayed there for one week and then flew back to e United States to start their life together. My other had never been to the US before then." ita focused on the parts of the story that had ways fascinated her, dangling them like shiny istractions in hopes they might stave off more robing inquiries from Jag. "Two years later, I as born, and three years after that my sister, adia, arrived. That's the lot of us, Mom, Dad, ister, uncles, cousins and me." She ended on a hipper note, her voice light and easy, even as er stomach turned over.

"Long-distance trucking? That's—once again, couldn't have come up with something better," e said.

"And why is that?" she asked, knowing sh
shouldn't.

"Not only are you a mechanic, but you com
from a line of blue-collar immigrants. While
know that immigrants grow and strengthen th
economy, it's not generally the population on
chooses a princess from. Among his many flaw:
my father is also a bigot. He despises Hayat's im
migrant population, who happen to be prima
ily of South Asian origin, like yourself, and wi
hate it even more that you come from immigran
American stock, in addition to your plethora o
perfectly imperfect traits. The common peopl
of Hayat, however, are going to love you, eve
as my father seethes!

"I assume," he said, moving on as if position
ing one's wife in opposition to one's father wa:
done every day, "that trucking is where your in
terest in mechanics and engineering came from?"

Nodding, Rita said, "Yeah. Cars, and trucks
and things that go. I was all about them from ar
early age. Honestly, it was all I was ever interested in. My dad took me on drives with him
every summer as soon as I was old enough to no
need a car seat. Those were my favorite."

Examining her, he said, "It is easy to imagine
you as a little child in a big truck."

Rita laughed. "When I was really small, before the drives, I had to sit on a stack of telephone
books just to see through the window."

"Telephone books?" he asked.

Holding back her laugh, she said, "Telephone books were these old things that used to hold the phone numbers of area people and businesses."

"They just gave that information away for free?" Jag asked, shocked. "That seems like a breach of privacy," he added.

Laughing now, Rita said, "Things were different back in the Wild West days of America, especially when you were not royal," she said. "You had to ford rivers and use wired telephones."

Smiling, he indulged her joke, saying gravely, "The hardships you've endured," before shaking his head as he said again, more to himself, "Long distance trucking."

Rita rolled her eyes, relieved more than irritated to be in the safe territory of discussing her family's trucking history.

In truth, her family was never far from her mind, but as her life as NECTAR had blossomed, she had arrived at a place of balance in which thoughts of them operated in the background rather than as a constant grievance at the forefront.

Dinner tonight with the Prince, however, had pushed them back to the surface, if only because it had reminded her once again of what it was like to be a part of a unit.

Their unit might only be just the two of them, but even with all of the restrictions and stipula-

tions they were operating under, they had st
managed to form a team of sorts.

For better or worse, their bond was growi
stronger, drifting, if not toward a true marriag
then precariously far from simply being a pair
colleagues involved in a business deal.

But perhaps most dangerous of all, thorny co
versations included, tonight's dinner had forc
Rita to recognize what she'd been unwilling
admit over the past week: she wanted more, a
she wanted it with Jag.

CHAPTER SEVEN

Ten days later

"This is quite the event you have going on here," Vincenzo Moretti, the current ruler of the European nation of Arista, said as Jag entered the room where the three men that meant more to him than any other living beings stood.

Pushing aside the image of Rita that filled his mind in contradiction of the idea, Jag opened his arms to Vincenzo, a true smile coming to his face for the first time that day.

"Brutal and monstrous my father may be," Jag said, "but he has an unfortunate affinity for making money. It is my only joy, then, to spend it lavishly."

Vin's father, the former King of Arista, had not been so gifted.

Like Jag's father, the man had lived as if his pleasure was the only important truth. And, like Jag's father, cruelty to their wives had been a pleasure that both Jag's and Vin's fathers shared.

"You couldn't have found a little more useful pet project, Jag? A hospital, for instance, seems perhaps more practical than the 'world's largest biophilic structure'?" Rafael asked without hope, knowing Jag well enough to know the question to be pointless.

"I've completed six state-of-the-art hospitals within the past three years. No one in Hayat City lives more than twenty minutes from a brand-new, fully equipped hospital. I wanted to treat myself, as they say in America."

With a scoff, Zeus said, "Since when did you begin dabbling in American aphorisms?"

It would be Zeus, Jag thought with a mental sigh, to pinpoint the unconscious revelation in a statement.

When a matter needed to be cut through with a heavy, relentless tool—something powerful enough to shatter and destroy any attempt at obfuscation and illusion—it was always Zeus.

The Aegean Prince was a living broadsword.

With these men who knew him so well, there was no point in or need for deflection or hedging.

"Since I made an American woman my bride," Jag answered openly.

It was as if the very room in the secure downtown office sucked in its breath then, freezing the three men within it in a moment of silence before all of them began speaking at once.

"You married?" from Rafael, a grimace ready n place across his swarthy visage.

"Who is she?" Vin asked.

"When do we meet this bride of yours? I assume she is as desperately unsuitable as planned?" Zeus drawled. Eyes lighting, he added, "Tell me she is hideous."

Jag said stiffly, "She is not."

With far greater restraint, Rafael suggested without sarcasm, "Her being an American is enough."

"Excuse you," Vin said testily, his own American bride likely on his mind.

"Then what is it that makes this bride of yours so unsuitable? Or is she not? Did you go and fall into the same love trap as the rest of us?" Zeus asked.

Waving Zeus's words away, Jag said, "Oh, no. My bride is most perfectly unsuitable. And we are most certainly not in love. She's a mechanic from Oakland."

The three men in the room burst into laughter.

"It seems you're the only one of us who made it, chap," Zeus said, laughter lingering in his eyes.

Even Rafael chimed in, a thread of rare amusement lightening his voice. "While there is nothing wrong with being a mechanic," he said, "it certainly isn't a background that would prepare one for ruling a nation."

Vin's voice and smile were rueful when he

said, "I would have liked to welcome you to our side of this game, friend, but I must admit it sounds like, of all of us, you may be the only one to have fulfilled the terms of our agreement so thoroughly."

With a smile devoid of humor, Jag said, "It would appear so…"

"But? I sense a but there." Zeus asked.

"Is she proving to be too unsuitable?" Rafael asked, ever astute.

Shaking his head, Jag said, "No. She is truly ideally unsuitable, a study in contrasts really. She's reckless, and brash, and daring and foolhardy, but she's also shy and reserved. There is not a subtle thing about her body, and yet she excels at maintaining mystery and her own counsel. She's certifiably brilliant. Rarely have I encountered a mind as quick and discerning as hers. And, for the record, she is as far from hideous as it's possible to be. She represents everything my father hates while offering everything the people of Hayat could want in a princess. I could not have discovered a more perfectly imperfect woman if I had been trying. And I wasn't. I was just picking up my car."

"I'm beginning to see your problem," Zeus said dryly.

"As do I," said Rafael.

"Clear as day," Vin added.

"And just what is that?" Jag said testily, lifting

eyebrow, ready to deny whatever wild theo-
s they put forth.

Until Zeus said, simply, "You want her."

"That's absolutely absurd. Were you listening
what I said? She's utterly unsuitable."

"We heard the important part," Vin said with
grin.

"*Perfect* was the word I believe you used," Ra-
el added.

"Couldn't have discovered better if you'd been
ving," Zeus served his words back to him.

Jag closed his eyes and forcibly set down the
olent urge to deny it again.

His friends would never believe it, and nei-
er could he.

He *did* want Rita.

His want of her was an ever-increasing pres-
nce in the back of his mind, constantly growing
size like a monstrous tumor, threatening the
fe of the arrangement he had made with her as
ell, not to mention his own. He could not afford
) want anything, not like this. Not the kind of
ant that led to feelings and attachment. It was
o much of a risk.

No relationship could ever again become a tool
ith which he could be manipulated.

But he could no longer deny it. Not to these
en and not to himself.

"I want her," he said, lowering his head in defeat.
While his plans were by no means completely

devastated by his desire for Rita, he would be fool to deny that it put everything in jeopardy. was already too much that he had eaten dinne with her each night since the first, and that he' come to crave her company enough every da that he made excuses to ensure that it happenec

"So have her. So long as she wants you, too, Zeus egged on, ever the voice of the devil on hi shoulder. "Isn't that one of the few known bene fits to come with the baggage of matrimony?" h asked, as if he were not more than happy bein; burdened by the baggage of matrimony and fam ily himself.

"Did she reject you?" Rafael asked, his char acteristically bored tone lifting with the ring o real incredulity.

Jag wished there were space inside him to take pride in the thread of disbelief and doubt interwoven in his friend's question, but it didn't truly matter if there had never been a woman interested in denying him before if he could not have the woman that he shared a life with now.

Shaking his head, he said, "No. But I must keep my distance."

"Must." Zeus shivered with distaste. "Such an ugly word."

Jag agreed. "The only way this works is if Rita and I remain professional. Otherwise, she becomes a liability. This close to seeing things through with my father, there is no room for

rust and opening up. Not in Hayat. It was dif-
erent with the three of you. My father is on his
ome turf. If he were to sense even the slight-
st hint of emotion he would use that, and her,
gainst me."

A new seriousness coming into his voice, Ra-
ael said, "If you think that is even a possibility,
you must keep her as far from you as possible."

But Jag waved his warning away. "It's not. Not
with Rita. The woman doesn't have a grasping
bone in her body. All she wants to do is save
he world, one car at a time," he said, and if he
sounded exasperated by his own devil's advocacy
it was only because it was true.

He could not seem to stop going back and forth
when it came to Rita.

"If you're that certain, then once again I do not
see your problem," Zeus said. "You trust her, so
have her."

Incensed, Jag whipped toward his friend. "I
can't risk a kingdom on a hunch, Zeus!"

"I don't envy you your position," Vin said.

"It is rather sticky," Zeus added, unperturbed
by his friend's outburst.

"No, it's not," Rafael said. "It's clear what you
need to do. There is no challenge to it whatso-
ever. As you said, you can't risk a kingdom. Not
on a hunch, and not on pent-up desire, either.
Under no circumstances allow yourself to be
alone with her. All you need to do is remember

how long you've been implementing this pl:
how much you have sacrificed along the w:
the peace of your people, and what remains
the line while your father is still in power. A:
if that is not a strong enough deterrent, thi:
about your mother."

A bastard, as well as having served as rege
of his nation for his child half brother, far
ily ties—as well as mothers—were simult
neously fraught and rigid subjects in Rafae
world view.

Vin let out a laugh that sounded like a coug
"May we all be blessed with such self-contrc
Rafael. I know the three of us have not show
ourselves to be so endowed."

"Self-control is overrated," Zeus chimed i:
"All one truly needs is power."

"Well, power—" Jag grabbed on to the ide
like it was a lifesaver "—is something th:
I have in spades. Therefore, worry not, m:
friends. Today is not a day for ominous warr
ings. Today, I have the rare triple pleasures
visiting friends, enraging my father to the glor
of my nation, and announcing my marriage to
brilliant and beautiful woman. What more coul
a man want?"

"Well, I for one can't wait to meet the mor
that you want," Zeus said, at which Vin smile
and Rafael's eyes lit with humor.

Only briefly, Jag wondered if he needed friends as much as he'd thought.

After weeks now dedicated to putting together a showcase for her work at the exhibition, she could not believe it was all ready for the grand finale.

Her babies had done exceptionally on the world stage, her private fleet of vehicles making its world debut as if it had been born for the moment. Her inbox was overflowing with commission requests and she'd made some connections that she was excited might mean her dream was that much closer to becoming real.

And her baby, the astonishing car that she had been dreaming of her whole life until the day the Prince had sent it to her garage, the very catalyst for all of it, had eviscerated the competition in the all-electric race.

All of it had been better than she'd even imagined.

But now it was time to get ready for her debut.

Rita squeezed into the long black throat-to-ankle, shoulder-to-wrist bodysuit that Jameel had sent with mild trepidation.

Made of shimmering stretchy formfitting material that had the appearance of leather and the breathability of a mesh, the suit hugged every nook and cranny of her form, leaving little to the imagination.

The legs of the garment were accented with

diagonal motorcycle stripes across the thigh
and the overall impression it gave was one of
woman who had been born to ride and ready t
kick ass.

"I—I can't wear this," she stuttered. Sh
looked sexier than she ever had in her life.

This was not what one wore to debut to th
world.

And then she saw the accessories.

A belt made of pearls the size of baby's fists—
bigger than Rita had even known possible—
glowed in the living, breathing way that onl
pearls seemed able to do.

A chandelier necklace was obviously intende
to wrap around the turtleneck neckline of the
catsuit and drape decadently across her colla
and chest.

Stunning earrings matched the belt, with dia
mond posts and three pearls dangling below each

To the left in the case, a set of three intricately
filigreed diamond-encrusted tennis bracelets glit-
tered contentedly, and on the right was a lovely
diamond anklet with tiny tinkling platinum bells
swinging from it.

None of it, however, compared to the enormous
ring that lay in the center of it all.

Rita brought a hand up to cover her mouth,
equal parts horrified and amazed.

It was a ring fit for a princess—a ring fit to let

he world know she was a taken woman, and, if
y outrageous ostentatiousness alone, by whom.

Closing her eyes as she began to put it on, the
est of her senses attuned to the gentle pressure
f the jewelry as she lay it across her catsuit-
lad skin.

She could not see them yet, but she could sense
hat the jewels would be breathtaking—if only
rom the glare shining up from her chest.

She was beginning to wonder, however, when
nd how her outfit would transition from that of
a bedazzled femme fatale into that of a proper
nternational daughter-in-law making her debut.

And then she saw the overlayer.

An expanse of sheer fabric that shimmered in
he light, it was thick, yet transparent.

Most astoundingly, it was in a shade of blue
hat was an exact match to the iridescent paint
she had used on the Ferrari.

It was a long fitted jacket that buttoned up the
back, with enormous billowing bell sleeves that
gathered at the wrist just below where her bracelets rested.

When worn over the catsuit and jewels, what
had begun as a revealing outfit on the cutting
edge of fashion transformed into something mod-
est and chic.

And although the jacket obscured the view
of what lay beneath, because it was transparent
and eye-catching, and because the jewels beneath

shone through so clearly, it also begged the eye to look closer.

She somehow looked as ready for a spin around the racetrack as she did an elegant twirl around a ballroom.

Which was good, because it was time to go.

The car was waiting to shuttle her away to her grand debut.

Rita was to meet the Prince at a private entrance of the capital city's world-famous botanical gardens where the closing gala was taking place and the announcement would be made.

In no time at all, the driver was parking and walking around to open her door.

Taking his hand, she stepped out, finding the shoes surprisingly stable, easier to walk in than any heels she'd ever worn before.

She turned to thank the driver when a movement in the corner of her eye caught her attention.

It was Jag.

He had changed clothing as well.

No longer did he wear the full traditional Hayat-style clothing that he'd been wearing in the various photographs she'd seen of him from throughout the day, though he still wore his white ghutra and agal.

Paired with his bespoke suit, he was a sight to see.

The deep black of his suit set off the constantly burning fire in his eyes.

As always, he was captivating, commanding her attention and focus like a machine made for just that function.

His eyes shone as he took her in, gaze falling on her hand and, impossibly, flaring even more before returning to her face.

"Ravishing," he said.

The wonder in his voice worked its way around her heart and squeezed.

"Not so bad yourself," she said, awkwardly, wishing she had a greater lexicon for this moment than the one she'd picked up from romantic comedies.

Unfortunately, there was not another genre that would lend her vocabulary for the situation she found herself in.

What compliments did you give to a man who was your husband but not your lover?

What level of physical appreciation was appropriate with someone you were not allowed to be attracted to, but were?

How could she not be, when he looked like that? How could she resist when he was a force for his people who accepted nothing less than excellence from everyone around him, and gave back tenfold in response? Jag was dedicated, and shrewd, and hardworking, committed to providing the very best for those he was responsible for, and loyal to his core.

He was everything her mother would have told

her to hope for in a husband. The kind of perso
it was possible to fall in love with.

Rita didn't know how long they stood like tha
staring at one another, but it was long enoug
that it was a jolt to be reminded of what they ha
come here to do.

"Are you ready?" he asked, offering his arm

Was she ready? She wasn't sure it was pos
sible to be ready.

They were going in there to tell the world tha
she was his wife, and not only that, but that sh
was NECTAR.

And only half of it was true.

They might be married, but she was not hi:
wife.

Hands trembling faintly at her side, Rita shool
her head. This was a terrible idea.

"What's wrong?" he asked, concern deepen
ing the timbre of his voice as he drew her to
him, interlacing her chilled fingertips with his
warm ones.

"This isn't a good idea. We can't pull this off.
No one will ever believe the two of us are really
married."

Tilting her chin up, Jag faced her, expression
serious. "You are so brilliant and beautiful that
they will believe anything you tell them just for
a chance to be in the same room with you. You
don't go in there to be shamed, but to shine in
front of an adoring crowd. *Your* fleet was the

urprise hit of the exhibition, *your* car irrefut-
bly attested to the world the power and speed
otential of electric, and your reveal tonight is the
irst step in getting the world to reconsider how
 gets around. You're the star of this exhibition,
vhether the world knows you are or not. We don't
ave to do this this way, Rita. The results of the
xhibition were better than even expected. I can
lose the exhibition myself and we can create a
nore formal debut for our marriage with an al-
ered origin story. But you will never again have
nother opportunity like tonight with which to
tep on stage and transfix the globe. The choice
s yours, Rita."

Rita stared at him, unable to even settle on an
xpression, let alone a course of action. He was
willing to let her keep her secret identity but unwilling to let her off the hook.

Like her dad had been, before the whole
matching thing.

He would let her hide, but he wouldn't do it
without letting her know the consequences.

She knew Jag was right, not because he said
it, but because she herself had seen her reach ex-
pand over the course of the exhibition. Her work
had caught the attention of the international community.

What she did now would determine whether
they forgot about her as soon as her moment had

passed or stuck around to listen to what she ha
to say.

She had hidden behind NECTAR because pe
ple had not listened to what she had to say whe
they thought she was a woman. She had done
because women weren't supposed to do and li
and study what she did.

And now her strategy was threatening to b
come a different kind of silencer.

She had to trust that she was ready to hold h
own in front of the world. She had to trust Jag

But what if they rejected her? Could she hand
the wider public saying all the things her paren
had said about her hopes and dreams?

Squeezing her hand, Jag said in a low ton
"You've gone quiet."

Rita cleared her throat. Then clear and lou
and strong—as far a cry from the similar declar:
tion she had made sobbing to her parents so lon
ago—she said, "I choose to change the world.'

Jag's smile in response was beyond blindin
and it occurred to Rita that, though he had bee
willing to let her lead, it had been his dreams an
plans that had been on the line as well.

"You will blow them all away, Rita. None o
them will know what hit them, even as they wil
be desperate for more—not the press, the peo
ple of Hayat, nor the heads of the industries yo
will transform." He held her hand as he spoke

squeezing again before he asked her quietly, "Are you ready to become a national pride and joy?"

Chuckling to herself, the sound bubbling up to burst through some of the anxiety, she squeezed his hand in response and nodded. "I am," she said.

Not everyone was going to love her, she knew.

Her father-in-law was somewhere in the crowd tonight.

But that was also her part in their arrangement, and she was prepared.

Tonight would mark the first time she met the man in person, but having gone nearly four weeks in residence in Hayat, she had now seen his image enough times to know what he looked like.

Jag had warned her to expect that her father-in-law would be nasty, reminding her that the man was a ruthless tyrant even as recently as the last dinner they'd shared.

Having her own history of nasty encounters with fathers, Rita could handle herself.

She would be everything Jag needed her to be, when it came to his father and the public. It was the least she could give in return for the man who not only supported who and what she was but also believed in her capacity to push both toward achieving her dreams.

Stepping through this door represented entering into a new future, for all that Jag hadn't asked her to change herself.

It was a dangerous future in which the world knew who she was.

It was a future as the wife of the man at her side.

There was no going back once everyone knew.

Looking up at Jag, she was once again caught by the fiery amber of his gaze.

Something tormented and pained struggled in his look, his lips taking on an unfamiliar grimace as he opened them to force out the words, "Last chance to turn back."

Shaking her head, Rita said, "No. That moment passed. We're in it together. Let's do this."

Relief returned Jag's face back to the confident mask she was coming to know so well, and he nodded. Then he opened the door.

Rita gasped.

Massive walls of green glass arched overhead and around.

Stepping into the room, she walked into a wall of humidity, the perfumed air thick and moist in the room despite the ventilation provided by the many open windows.

Being inside it was as if she had stepped into a prehistoric jungle.

The room housed three long shallow rectangular pools each graced with lily pads, lotuses and other gorgeous water plants that Rita had not come across in any of her gardening classes.

Partygoers dotted walkways, standing on small arched bridges, swirling glasses of effervescent liquid while tuxedo-clad servers replenished drinks and handed out hors d'oeuvres.

As she gained her bearings, Jag scanned the crowd, his eyes coming to rest on a group of white-clad men in a far corner.

Though they were far away, Rita could just make out the features of the man who was her father-in-law.

She swallowed, and once again Jag squeezed her hand.

"I will keep you safe," he promised, reading her accurately.

And because he had already done the most important thing of making it safe to be the woman she was—with the interests she had and the goals she wanted to achieve—she believed he would.

But he was mistaken if he thought it was his father that she feared most tonight.

Resolute or not, she was most afraid of coming out to the world.

But there was no more time to worry.

With a signal to a server, Jag indicated it was time.

The man lifted a glass and clinked a fork against its side with enough force to cast its tinkling sound out and over the crowd.

That such a small sound, in a sea of noise and chatter, had the power to catch the attention of so many people was just one of the many mysteries of life.

As Rita watched, a wave of calm focus descended upon the attendees, each of them turning their faces toward the sound of the glass only to land upon the Prince of Hayat and Rita at his side.

"Good evening, ladies and gentlemen," Jag began. "After two weeks of astonishing sights and sounds, and the out-of-this-world race of tonight, it hardly seems fathomable that more excitement could emerge from this exhibition."

A light cheer rose in response to his words, with more than a few lifting glasses, before he continued, "But I would not be the Prince of Hayat—" he paused, allowing time for another small round of applause, before continuing "—if I let such a grand event close without an even grander finale."

More applause met his words, and Rita's stomach did a flip.

With each word, they drew closer to the point of no return.

"And I assure you, what I share with you now has been worth the wait."

The silence of rapt attention greeted him.

"You have all been dying to know, how did that rascally Prince get his hands on so many of NECTAR's custom specials? Well, here is your swer." Raising Rita's left arm, ensuring that ∶ massive ring she wore caught and refracted ∶ light, Jag said, "I present to you, revealed for ∶ first time to the world, the ingenious and in‐ mparable NECTAR. She is the woman who s blessed me by becoming my wife, Princess ta of Hayat."

Deafening cheers and a blitz of flashing lights eeted his announcement, and it was all Rita uld do to maintain her grip on his hand and ile for the cameras.

ours that felt like lifetimes later, Jag was hot d ready to have Rita back as his private trea‐ re.

In the past weeks he had gotten used to enjoy‐ g her company alone.

And while both the debut and exhibition had ne exactly as he had intended them to—bet‐ r even—he realized he was ready for things to t back to the normal they were establishing.

Introducing her as his wife as the finale of the hibition after revealing her to be the infamous ECTAR, drawing in the flare of romance and trigue while his attendees were already roll‐ g high on the exciting cocktail of enthusiasm r electric energy and innovation and fast cars, ade for exactly the instant sensation he had esired.

He would have final data back only following to‐

night's grand finale, but the preliminary information his team was sending him even now showed
that the exhibition and announcement of his marriage had had exactly the impact he wanted.

Rita had handled it all like she had been born
for it, including the media.

"How did the two of you meet?" one reporter
had asked, while others shouted out their own
queries. "Tell us about yourself, Princess Rita.
Who are you? Where are you from?"

"How long have you known each other?" still
another asked, and so it went for the rest of the
evening.

Rita navigated it with grace equal to that of
her stunning beauty.

Jag was used to being the center of attention
in a room, to being constantly in demand and
fielding personal questions, to graciously smiling when asked for selfie after selfie.

Rita, however, was new to all of it. And yet
she handled it with open warmth that only added
to her charm.

"I'm from California," she answered one, before adding, "in the US."

And when she was asked the follow-up question of, "But where's your family *really* from?"
Jag was impressed by the diplomacy with which
she answered.

"If you mean ancestrally," she said, "my grand-
parents immigrated to the United States from

Bangladesh. My father was born in the US, as was I, but my mother is Bengali."

Enraptured, the reporter said, "Now that you are Princess, do you feel that you're going to bring greater visibility to the large South Asian population living here in Hayat?" and belatedly Mag realized that he and Rita had spent very little time discussing the history, politics and realities of Hayat.

But Rita did not need his help.

"Of course," she said. "It is an honor to be a woman of South Asian descent and to bring representation of South Asians to a higher level here in Hayat. As an American, I have a lot to learn about the complex history and people of Hayat, but for now, I'm just glad that my presence brings greater visibility to such an important national demographic."

The woman took his breath away. How was it that he had only known her for a matter of weeks, when she stood by his side as if she had been training for the role? She was so much more than the perfectly imperfect sensation of a bride that he had thought he found in a Northern California garage. Over and over she had proved to him that she was not a ruse, with each new facet he encountered more evidence that she was, in fact, actually perfect.

Had their announcement been authentic, had she been the love that swept him away in every

sense of the world, at this moment, Jag wou[ld]
have been the proudest man on earth.

Even still, he knew there was no better choi[ce]
in all of the world.

And that was a real shame, because for all
her perfection, his union with Rita was temp[o]
rary.

She was not his wife. She was not his quee[n.]

Their paths would separate in the near f[u]
ture—must separate—and when they did, the[re]
would be no one who could ever stand a chan[ce]
of replacing her.

Stepping closer in a show of their affecti[on]
and unity, as well as to savor the nearness th[at]
was as close as he could get, Jag cultivated a mi[s]
chievous twinkle in his eye and said, "You mu[st]
all forgive me. My darling wife swept me awa[y]
in such a whirlwind that it has been all I cou[ld]
do to keep her to myself up to now. Our une[x]
pected romance coinciding with this exhibitio[n]
has given me little time to introduce my brid[e]
to the complexities of Hayati history. But with
mind like hers, I am sure it will only be a ma[t]
ter of time before she becomes a better nation[al]
representative than even I."

They chuckled in response to his words, an[d]
he led Rita away, directing them toward the sma[ll]
group of men that made up the full list of peop[le]
he trusted in the world.

If she was not his forever, she was at least hi[s]

for now, and if it had been real, this would have been a moment he eagerly anticipated.

He watched his friends as their gazes landed on Rita, more eager and proud to introduce them to his bride than he should have been.

In a way, it had been them who had brought the two of them together—and their long-ago pact.

Zeus smiled first, eyes alighting with masculine delight on Rita. "You must be the bride we've heard so much about," he said. "I begin to see what has blown our friend in such a wildly new direction."

Smiling, Rita offered her hand. "The blowing is mutual, I assure you. I certainly never expected to end up here."

At Zeus's side, Vin choked, quickly taking a sip from the champagne flute he held

Catching his eye over Rita's head briefly, Zeus replied to her, "Probably not as mutual as Jag would like."

And Vin quickly came in with, "What Zeus means is that no man is truly prepared for the moment that a transformative woman enters his life and changes everything he ever imagined for himself."

At this, Rita narrowed her eyes, though Jag was grateful for his friend's smooth cover.

Tilting her head to the side, still eyeing them closely, she asked, "You must be the 'few men I

call friends' that I keep hearing about?" pitchin
her voice as she mimicked Jag.

All of the air fled from Jag, not for fear thei
conversation would be overheard—her word
were easy enough to explain away—but at he
directness. Of course, Rita wouldn't beat aroun
the bush with the men he had told her she di
not need to.

With a small chuckle, Rafael spoke up finally
"We are, indeed."

Looking from man to man before settling he
gaze on Zeus, one of her eyebrows lifted, she saic
saucily, "Well then, isn't it just so nice to be in
company where we can speak freely."

A bolt of pride jolted through Jag at her, as she
showed no signs of being intimidated by these
men who controlled nations. Not many dared to
meet them head-on.

Laughing openly, Zeus agreed. "It is, indeed,
Princess. And, speaking freely, I can say that it
is truly a delight to make your acquaintance. I
have no doubt, you will drive our friend Jag here
to absolute distraction."

"Let us just hope that distraction is not synon-
ymous with ruin," Jag said, pitching his voice jo-
vially as another group of reporters neared them,
mics at the ready.

Taking Jag's cue for the warning it was, his
friends shifted their bodies into their royal public personas as the media arrived.

Jag noted a murmur running through the crowd of reporters and knew the time for light inquiries had come to an end. His father had finally made his move.

Jag brought an arm around Rita's shoulders protectively before gently turning her to face his father, himself offering the man a nod of the head that was just shy of respectful.

"Father," he said, watching him closely.

The helpless rage that boiled in his father's eyes was of an intensity unparalleled in Jag's experience, and a part of him thrilled.

Learning that his son had married without his consent or input this way, in a public forum after the fact, and that his daughter-in-law and the future Queen of his country was all of the things he despised in modern women, was nowhere near the shock and pain that Jag himself had felt when he'd learned what had happened to his mother, but it was enough that it felt good.

It was a start.

Staring at his father, seeing his rage all the while knowing that his plan to take the only thing that had ever mattered to him—just as his father had done to him, so long ago—had begun in earnest, was the closest thing to justice that Jag had ever felt.

And this was only the beginning of a grand scheme that had started with an electric exhibition and an unexpected daughter-in-law and would end in prison.

Jag's blood sang, his eyes lighting with the satisfaction of things going exactly according to plan.

His father refused to look at Rita, averting his eyes upward for all the impression he gave of gazing at her with fatherly love and affection.

Rita was everything that his father detested in a woman: smart, ambitious, hardworking and bold.

And though he had learned of his son's matrimonial status for the first time tonight, like everyone else in attendance, the King would have to pretend that he had not only known but approved, when in fact he had not even given his blessing—that was an immense disrespect.

But the worst of the situation would have been the arrangements and concessions his father would have to give to whomever he had already promised Jag's hand in marriage to. Jag had no doubt that his father had always intended to select a bride for him, and a bride who would be a benefit to himself—not Jag nor the people of Hayat.

By making his announcement so painfully public, his father was forced to play along or lose face. It was no less than he deserved.

And his father knew that Jag meant every bit of it.

"My son!" His father's voice was booming and

vial, the size of it intended to dominate for all
at he sounded harmless.

The room quieted.

"You have outdone yourself as ever with your
stounding exhibition, global leadership and
ommitting Hayat to a one hundred percent elec-
ic society within the next fifty years. As in ev-
rything, you have proved once again that the
nnovation and style and groundbreaking lead-
rship of Hayat is boundless."

Muted applause followed his father's remarks
nd his eyes—the same burning brown orbs that
tared at Jag in his own mirror—sharpened,
lued to Jag's face as he spoke, conveying threat
nd fury even as his face presented geniality.

Jag angled further toward Rita, placing his
ody between hers and his father's.

Turning, his father finally addressed her. "My
aughter," he said, a hint of poison in the word.
Your unbelievable achievements are living proof
hat even the lowliest can climb to great heights
vhen given the example and trappings of quality.
Through your toil you have earned the attention
nd affection of my son. Your accomplishments
re a testament to our house."

While those gathered applauded, Jag did not.

He had anticipated an encounter like this, had
ooked forward to it even, but he had not ac-
counted for his own reaction to his father's tak-
ng aim at Rita.

He had not anticipated that he would be fille
with the urge to tear his father apart.

Beside him, Rita gave Jag's hand the faintest o
squeezes—enough to remind him that he neede
to get himself under control.

Unable to let the insult slide completely unad
dressed, however, Jag said, "Come now, Fathe
You and I both know that it is Rita who redirect
our jaded and capitalist eyes toward the thing:
which truly matter. It is her heart that is beating
new life into the house of Hayat."

Again, Jag was rewarded by his father's glare
that meant the barb had hit its mark.

Cheeks reddening, his father opened his
mouth, no doubt to issue another disparaging re-
mark, when Rita startled them both, her bright
smile and fearless American accent tromping
right into the fray like a lost tourist. "We must
give the credit where it is truly due. It is family
that teaches us—" and here she looked up at Jag.
her eyes sparkling as she put on an outstanding
performance of a blushing new bride "—that it
is only through learning together that we ever
truly discover anything."

The room burst into boisterous applause.

She was incredible.

Jag swallowed, and in the action regained his
center, or perhaps more accurately, recentered
with her.

In the lighting and humidity, she was big-eyed

nd dewy and hopeful—a princess the world ould love—and she had completely stolen the potlight from both himself and his father.

He couldn't think of another woman in the world who could have done it better.

He was ready to have her to himself.

Fortunately, one of the perks of being a prince vas leaving when you wanted to.

Lifting Rita's arm while the applause died lown, Jag announced, "We are sorry to say farevell, my friends, but after two weeks of electric mania, an exhilarating race and this wonderful party, I am afraid I must whisk my bride away."

The room let out a collective sigh of disappointment, and Jag had to stop himself from smiling. His father did not have a chance against Rita.

It was slow going, making their way out in an endless parade of additional waves and farewells, but he and his newly revealed princess made their way through the red-carpeted main entrance of the botanical gardens to the driveway where the valet waited for them, holding open the door of the Ferrari.

Rita sucked in an audible breath, a bright smile coming to her face. "You had a fresh set of rubber put on," she said, cheeks darkening.

He laughed. Only Rita would comment on tires. But beneath the words, there was a trill of real excitement, and he knew he'd made the right choice.

"After you, Princess." He had not intended to draw the word out, to make it into a sensual caress, bold and telling when uttered while staring into her eyes.

Her lips parted and then closed again as she swallowed, rapt and otherwise frozen.

And then she blinked, as if snapping out of a spell, and licked her lips with a fleeting frown that disappeared as soon as her eyes returned to the car. Her gaze cleared and she took a deep breath, smiling before she slid into the passenger seat.

Taking the keys from the valet as he walked around the front, he got into the driver's seat beside her.

"You're driving?" she asked, surprised.

He sighed, drawing out the sound though he felt no real irritation. She could question the obvious as much as she wanted, so long as she never stopped being her open and honest self with him. "Did you think I was going to ride in the back?"

"I've just never seen you drive before," she pushed, and he laughed.

"Well, then, you're in for a treat. I hope you like to go fast."

Lighting up like a star in the sky, she answered though she didn't have to. "Do I ever."

Laughter extending, Jag shook his head as he turned the system on.

He loved it when she spoke like a character from a film.

And then they were off, her squealing in delight the whole way.

CHAPTER EIGHT

Some women loved expensive gifts. Some women loved cuddly things. Rita loved cars.

Jag raced through the streets of Hayat City at unconscionable speeds, dashing past unbothered police officers and through lights that were somehow always miraculously green. Rita's heart thundered and her body felt skin-tinglingly alive.

The man could drive.

He drove fearlessly and with purpose, and it was everything she could do not to stare at his profile at the wheel.

The car, the man—it was nearly too much.

And then they were abruptly outside the city, racing down a long stretch of night-dark freeway hugged on either side by smooth dunes of sand and tucked beneath a blazing quilt of stars.

And that was when he really got going.

Like a bolt of lightning, they struck out into the desert at blazing speed.

In what felt like the blink of an eye, they were

alone on the road, just the two of them cradled in the car of her dreams.

Rita couldn't hold back the sigh of contentment that escaped her lips.

Jag looked over at her then, just for an instant before he turned back to the road, but there had been enough heat in his gaze to burn her to ash.

Ever so gradually beginning to slow, his fingers flexed around the steering wheel.

Licking her lips to moisten them, Rita asked, "Where are we going?"

Taking her offer of small talk, he answered, "I'm merely taking us home, the long way. There is something I thought you might like to see out here, but mostly, I thought you'd like taking the baby."

Heat coming to her cheeks, she gave a self-deprecating laugh. "I do. More than I probably should. Thank you."

Having slowed to a normal cruising speed, Jag had time to scan her before he said, "There is nothing wrong with loving cars, Rita. I do. I don't know if you know this about me, but I have been known to spend exorbitant—dare I say extortionate—rates for vehicles."

Rita snorted, comforted even if she didn't want to be, but outside, she retorted, "Some things are priceless," as she stroked the dashboard that she'd spent hours of her life lovingly restoring.

Jag noted the motion of her hand, watching it

for a moment with an intensity at odds with the cockiness of his voice as he said, "I've heard that said, though I've never found it to be so."

She rolled her eyes. "It must be good to be a prince."

"If you don't mind the King," he said, a mixture of bitterness and heat in his voice.

Shuddering, Rita made a face of distaste thinking about the man who was her father-in-law. "I have to admit, he was worse than you described," she said.

"Unfortunately, it is hard to encapsulate his brand of ill will," he said flatly.

Waiting a beat, she asked, "Why do you hate him so much—I mean, beyond his being so obviously hateful?"

For a long time, he didn't say anything, simply stared at the road ahead.

When he finally spoke, his voice was dry and cracked, sounding older than he was.

"My mother was born in Egypt, but her family is from rural Hayat," he began. "She was beautiful, and kind, and smart. She loved horses and handbags."

"And you?" Rita guessed, now more certain than ever that it had been his mother who had given Jag his heart.

Closing his eyes, Jag agreed, "And me." After drawing in a choppy breath, he picked up again.

nd at one time, she loved my father. But the feel-
g died long before he took me away from her."

Knowing the pain of separation, Rita ached
r him. "I'm so sorry, Jag."

Shaking his head as if he could shake off her
ncern, he said, "He played us against each
her. He sent me to boarding school and would
e access to her to manipulate me into being the
n he wanted. Any transgression could mean the
ss of a visit or phone call, so I became perfect.
on, even perfect was not enough, however. For
ars, he would set impossible standards, know-
g I would never be able to achieve them. I had
arly completed school, the model son, when I
arned that the reason for the change had been
at she had died. He hadn't wanted to lose his
argaining chip so he simply didn't tell me. She
ied by herself, and for that alone I would never
ave been able to forgive him, but he'd gone
irther than that. For years, he paid someone to
orge letters from her so that he could use our
orrespondence to spy on me. He let me write
tters to a ghost in order to mine my most pri-
ate thoughts and feelings."

Rita brought a hand to her mouth in horror.
Oh, Jag."

With a bitter face, he added, "And when I fi-
ally stepped into the role of Crown Prince, three
ears ago, I learned that the same cruel tactics he
sed on me, he had been using on the people of

Hayat. He loves nothing more than illegal sur
veillance and emotional deception. Except per
haps skimming from the top."

Rita's stomach roiled, her entire being sickened
by what Jag's father had done.

That a father could be so monstrously cruel
was nearly beyond belief. She might not have
believed it, in fact, had she not met the man her
self—had she not come to trust in the prince at
her side.

And in trusting, she gained greater understanding of why he had been so reticent to build
emotional connections.

How could he take the risk of caring when he
knew his father would stop at nothing to manipulate and control him?

As it had in her own life, love and closeness
had been coercive and overbearing forces in
his—chains with which to dominate, rather than
to hitch onto toward joy and fulfillment.

It might have been bloodthirsty and merciless
of her, but she wished her father-in-law everlast-
ing torment for the cruelty he had bestowed upon
his wife and child and people.

Rita shuddered again. The world would not
suffer when his reign ended—even if, from what
she could glean, these days it was close to a thing
in name only.

Jag, as she understood, had taken the bulk of
the functions of his government under his lead

already, as if for him, too, that day could not come soon enough.

"No inspiring words of forgiveness and hope?" Jag asked, attempting lightness while the lingering harsh rasp of his voice belied his efforts.

Shaking her head, Rita said, "None. If this were a movie, it would be the kind of situation that would warrant grandiose vengeance."

With a strained laugh, he said, "Is that so?" before side-eyeing and nudging her with a sly smile and alluding to her words from earlier in the evening, "Family is so important, after all."

He was joking, merely making fun reference to her earlier words, but the reminder was akin to being wrapped up tight in a wet blanket.

Like Jag, she was estranged from her family because the demands of their love had been too much to bear, but after hearing his story, how could she ever share?

She had thought her family's demands were unfair, but compared to Jag, they'd simply asked for the same kind of commitment from her that they had given.

They had made big sacrifices for the happiness of the whole. Demanding the same of her was a far cry from the deception and manipulation Jag's father had employed.

What would he think if he knew that she had walked away from her family in favor of chasing dreams?

Knowing that he had been so cruelly ripp
from his mother, would he think her spoiled a
wasteful for throwing away something as go
and precious and priceless as she had?

Her parents might have been unrelenting
their desire to mold her, and they may have n
fully understood the beat of her heart, but the
had always loved her.

That fact of that stood out in sharp contrast
Jag's experience.

From what she knew now, it seemed like th
only one who had ever loved Jag was his mothe
and unlike Rita's family, with whom reconcil
ation might still someday be possible, she wa
long gone.

"Rita." A serious note had come into Jag
voice, one at odds enough with the tone of th
moment that it shook her out of her wallowin
and had her glancing at him with a frown, he
eyebrows drawn together.

"What is it?" she asked. "What's wrong?"

"In a moment, I'm going to pull the car ove
I want you to take off your overcoat and wrap
around your head, then I want you to curl up i
the footwell. Do you understand?" His voice wa
forcibly calm, steady and even, and all the mor
unsettling for it.

"What's wrong? What's going on?" she asked
struggling to shrug out of her jacket in the nar
row confines of the car as she spoke.

Still staring straight ahead, he said, "We are directly in the path of an oncoming sandstorm."

He spoke as if he delivered the most mundane news…even as he carefully untucked the folds of his ghutra and removed his agal.

Following his lead, she wrapped the sheer jacket around her head, doubtful the flimsy thing would provide much coverage through one of nature's disasters but unwilling to freak out.

Jag was remaining calm. She could remain calm.

"Curl up as tightly as you can." His muffled voice came through his own layers of wrapping, and she did as he said.

And moments later, they were swallowed by a wall of sand.

The sound was incredible and horrible. A crescendo of scratching and scraping wind, punctuated here and there by the screeching of metal being bent against its will.

Sand pummeled them, somehow able to make its way inside the car and beneath her wrapped jacket, grains of it forcefully aggressive in their push to get into her mouth and ears and tightly shut eyes.

The roar continued, seemingly endless.

And then, blessedly, it was over.

Coughing, Rita struggled out of her curled position, crawling up to sit on the sand-covered seat that she had abandoned.

At her side, she could hear the sand shifting a
Jag moved as well.

With a cough of his own, Jag asked, "Are yo
all right?"

"I think so," Rita said, unwrapping the layer:
of her jacket from around her head and sending
a cascade of sand falling down all around her.

There was sand everywhere.

And not just sand, but dirt and bits of rock—
even nestled among the crooks and crevices o
her gargantuan jewelry.

Abruptly overwhelmed by the sensation o
drowning in sand, Rita reached for the door handle and pulled it open, stumbling out of the ca
amidst a river of sand and more coughing.

On the other side of the car, Jag did the same.

Upright, Rita began the process of shaking
the invasive grains out of all the places they had
bombarded.

Removing her hair tie, she bent forward, flip-
ping her hair over in the process to rake and comb
her fingers through it, shaking free as much sand
as she possibly could.

Like glitter, the rain of it seemed never-ending.

Finally, after reaching the limit on the amount
of rattling her brain could handle, Rita came upright, letting her now-loose, dusty black hair fall.
It tumbled freely over her shoulders and down
her mid-back.

Further examination and dusting of her peron, however, revealed that aside from the now-sand-encrusted over-jacket and collection of lightly sandy priceless accessories, her outfit had come through the harrowing experience not much worse for wear.

Whereas she wasn't sure she would ever get all the sand out of her ears, the catsuit had somehow prevented any and all sand from penetrating its barrier.

Saved from the well-known horror of copious amounts of grit in unmentionable places, Rita was more than glad to see that Jameel's fashion efforts had proved to be so practical.

The same could not be said for Jag.

"What are you doing?" she asked, though it was very clear that he was in the process of removing his shirt, dexterously unbuttoning it from the top down. Strangled panic gripped Rita's throat, squeezing as her eyes locked on the motion of his deft fingers quickly working their way down the fastened column.

"What does it look like?" he said, not looking at her from his task. "I'm getting out of this sand-sodden clothing."

"And into what?" she croaked.

Rolling his eyes, he said dryly, "Why, into the change of clothes you can see that I packed."

He was being sarcastic. She knew it. There were no clothes in the Ferrari.

"You're just going to go naked?" she said,

panic rising. He couldn't go naked. Outside of images, Rita had never seen a naked man.

"Men have been known to go without clothing," he noted, amusement at her obvious embarrassment overwhelming his earlier irritation.

She knew that, rationally.

He had to disrobe to shower, and she didn't imagine he had been born wearing clothing.

But that didn't mean that she was prepared to be around him in all of his naked glory.

Heat coming to her cheeks, she whirled around, turning her back to him as she belatedly gave him the privacy she should never have breached.

"I'm so sorry," she said.

"For what?" He chuckled. "The fact that my ensemble doesn't appear to be as sealed as your own?"

"N-no," she stammered.

"Then what is it, Rita?" he asked, a wicked smile in his tone. "Or have you never seen a naked man before?"

"No," she lied. "I just shouldn't have looked. Our agreement..." She trailed off.

"That's right," he said, irritation once more bringing stiffness to his voice. "Our agreement. I haven't forgotten our agreement, Rita. You need not worry that my lack of clothing represents anything beyond an effort to prevent chafing. It will get chilly soon, though. The place I wanted

show you is nearby. We can stay warm there
hile we await assistance."

"Assistance?" Rita questioned, turning to
ace him in her surprise. "We aren't going to
st drive?"

But by the time the words had left her mouth
he was no longer interested in the answer.

Her mouth went dry.

She wanted to blame the dust and sand, but
hat storm had already passed—and had nothing
o do with a storm whipping up inside her now.

Jag stood glistening in the moonlight, shirtless,
he fastens of his pants undone, the front folds
anging open. His chest and arms were all mus-
led and gleaming strength, as perfectly formed
s any automotive frame she had ever laid eyes
n.

Curling hair dotted his pectorals before disap-
earing among the lines of rigid definition that
nade up his abdominals, only to reappear below
is belly button, this time marching in a straight
ine that led downward and disappeared beneath
he top fabric line of his boxers.

Rita swallowed hard, her entire focus attuned
o that line of fabric, her breath coming shallow
n her breast.

She had been aware of the fact that Jag was
andsome, had noticed how well he filled out his
lothing, his hard body a rigid form so perfect it
eemed to have been made for the task.

But she'd had no idea that beneath the perfect tailoring and exquisite materials lay a body that was enough to put the works of the great Renaissance masters to shame.

His skin was the exact shade of a perfect white mocha, creamy with a hint of tan, and in the bright moonlight, it glowed as much as the pearl belt she wore.

When she tore her eyes away from his body, yanking them back up to his face, what she saw there stole her breath all over again.

She was used to the eternal burning flame of his eyes, but the fires she saw now raged out of control, hotter than she had ever seen them.

And yet she had the sense that touching those flames would not bring her harm, but the opposite, in fact—the promise of immense pleasure.

Where such an idea came from, she had no idea.

No experience thus far in her life had prepared her for this moment with Jag.

With his gaze glued to her face, his hands came to the top of his pants.

Gasping, Rita ripped her gaze away from him once more, desperate for anything to take her mind off the growing heat in her body.

Casting out for anything to save herself, her eyes landed on the sand-buried form of the Ferrari, and for the millionth time that evening, her mood swung from one extreme to another.

Freed from the entrancement of seeing Jag's near-naked body, Rita now understood exactly why he said they would be waiting for assistance.

The Ferrari had been sheared by the sand, its light blue paint stripped in a flash by nature's cruel buffering.

Chipped-out spots, divots left by bits of rock and sand, dotted its surface until the hood resembled a cheese grater.

A massive spiderweb crack crossed the windshield diagonally from corner to corner.

Instead of a grille, there was now a solid brick of sand.

Fist coming to her mouth with a gasp she could not hold back, Rita's stomach knotted even as her mind continued to catalog the damage.

Dropping into a crouch, she examined the dust and sand-packed undercarriage. She had never seen sand as thick and solid as a brick wall before.

The excessive particulate must also be why her own eyes could not seem to stop welling over.

It wasn't because the car that she had dreamed up alongside her father so long ago and waited so long to bring to life was already gone, its life even shorter than the amount of time that she had spent as her father's pride and joy, all of its beauty and flair stripped and gone with just a shell left behind.

She did not look over when Jag crouched be-

side her, could not look away from the wreckage
even as she sensed the heat and nearness of his
presence and could catch the sandalwood scent
of his skin on the wind.

He was fully naked now, she knew it without
looking, but being unsettled by his nudity seemed
suddenly childish and unimportant when faced
with the wreck of the car.

Her tears fell just as Jag's arm came around
her shoulders.

The feeling of warm pressure of his bare skin
through the thin material of her suit unleashed
the floodgates.

Great racking sobs coursed through Rita's
body as she leaned into him. And he just let her
cry—for the pain of having to choose between
family and future, for the loss of the magnificent
car, and for the complications that kept them from
being everything to each other that they could.

When finally her tears had subsided, Jag's
voice was low and gentle when he said, "We
should go. We're not far from the place I wanted
to show you. We can walk there and call for assistance where it's warmer."

Gently, he drew her to her feet, and the movement, coupled with the reminder of his nudity
inevitably drew her eyes downward toward the
apex of his thighs, where a great mystery of the
world lay revealed to her.

As if powerless to the thrall of her hormones

and force of her curiosity, Rita could not look away as he stood before her riveted gaze.

Fiery heat flamed her cheeks, but she couldn't tear her eyes away.

Free from the cover of his clothing, the trail of hair that began beneath his belly button could be seen leading in a straight line to the dark hair at the base of his shaft.

She took note of the details of him as if she had never before seen a human body.

And perhaps she never had.

She certainly had never seen a body like Jag's.

Swallowing once more, her arm reached toward him without her say-so or permission, as if driven by a need all of its own. And, as if the small, unintended motion were enough to break the heavy spell that had entrapped them, Jag cleared his throat loudly and stepped back, severing the connection that held their gazes.

"We should get to the ruins," Jag said thickly, adding, "The desert cold catches one quicker than you'd imagine. Just give me a second to shake these out." The last was said as he rummaged through the pile of clothes that she had been certain only moments before that he was going to leave beside the wreck to retrieve the small black cloth of his boxers.

Looking away as he pulled them on, not cold in the least, Rita said, her voice viscous and heavy, knotting and tangling in her throat in the jumble

of all of the erotic details her eyes had taken in,
"Absolutely. Certainly. Take your time, it's fine.
Being comfortable is the most important." She
had to force herself to stop talking, realizing the
stream of repetitive assertions would only continue if she let it.

Stepping away as if even a little more space
would magically render her unaware of the powerfully attractive man she was with, she asked
with determined casualness, "Which direction?"

Eyeing her for a moment before answering, Jag
lifted an arm, pointed in a direction that looked
the same as every other direction in Rita's eyes,
and said, "That way."

Nodding decidedly, uncomfortably aware of
every private feminine place that the sight of her
naked husband had activated, her new sensual
alertness only further exacerbated by the intimate hug of her catsuit, Rita took a determined
step in the direction Jag had pointed, angling her
body and face so that his was just outside her line
of vision. Even now, clad in boxers, he was too
much stimulation. "Great. Let's go."

Behind her, Jag laughed. "Don't forget your
jacket. We're going to need it."

Stopping in her tracks, Rita returned to the car
to retrieve the jacket.

The walk was short, thankfully for Rita, who
soon followed behind Jag trying to look at the
stars, and the miles of dunes all around them, and

her shoeless feet sinking in the sand, and anything but the rear end of the man who led the way.

Dragging her eyes back up to the round and full moon overhead once more, Rita asked, "Where are we going again?"

"You'll see soon," Jag answered enigmatically.

"I had no idea there was a destination out this way," she noted.

"It's something not many people know about. I wanted to show you," he said.

Shortly thereafter, Rita wondered no more.

Appearing almost out of nowhere was a small ruin mound, its ancient stone walls crumbling into the dune that had built up around it, filling and burying parts of it, furthering the erosive process of the structure and the sand becoming one and the same.

In the bright moonlight, the ruin's arched doorways and crumbling pillars cast long dark shadows, only enhancing the sense that magic and mystery lurked all around.

A copse of date palms grew nestled into its shaded side, hidden from view by the direction from which they had approached the ruin, lending a sense of life to what otherwise might have seemed a lonely home for ghosts.

The shadowed beige of the stone blended seamlessly into the color of the sand around it, giving everything the impression not of an ancient structure, but of one built to match the existing landscape.

Impossibly drawn, Rita stepped toward the nearest doorway, fearless, led by her curiosity to see what lay inside.

Jag's hand on her shoulder stopped her.

"Another time," he said, "and in daylight."

Startled, as she always was by the experience of having another person weigh in on one of her decisions, Rita's face made a moue of disappointment, but she nodded.

What he said made sense.

She didn't know anything about what the desert held or what might be waiting inside the dark for her.

Leading her by the arm, Jag took her toward a crumbling staircase that led up to the flat square rooftop of a sand-filled rectangular structure.

Her bare feet touched the warm stones with relief, some of their chill dissipating instantly.

As usual, Jag's next two words indicated his preternatural ability to read her mind. "The stones heat up during the day and hold on to the heat long into the night."

Rita nodded. It made sense, and for a much more comfortable experience in the nighttime desert.

On the rooftop, Jag laid Rita's jacket on the ground. Then, beckoning her to come to his side, he lay down on his back, his arms under his head.

Rita sat down and joined him in lying back to look at the stars overhead.

They lay there, alone in the world and quily together for a time before Rita reluctantly minded him, "Weren't you going to call some-ne?"

He nodded but made no move for the phone at he had carried through the desert and which ow lay at his side. "Soon enough. I'm finding, owever, right now, amidst the oddity and dis-omfort of our situation, an unexpected feeling f peace. I want to enjoy it a little longer."

There was a quiet vulnerability in his voice, nd Rita didn't know why, but something about ie words warmed her.

While she couldn't take credit for the sand-orm, and wouldn't want to, she had had a part 1 creating this moment beneath the stars with iii, and even facing the devastation of the Fer-ari, she sensed that that was an accomplishment.

"What are you thinking about, my princess?" e asked, ever alert to her energetic and mental hifts.

With a sad chuckle, Rita sighed. "The car is uined."

Jag shrugged, saying, "I'll get you a new one."

This time Rita's laugh was incredulous. "You an't just get me a new one," she said. "There are nly so many of them in the world. And that one vas one-of-a-kind."

"It will be one-of-a-kind again when you re-build it, as I know you will," he said, uncon-cerned. "And I will still get you another one."

Smiling, Rita said, "You know, there is such a thing as having too much money." She was wear-ing the pearl belt, and chandelier necklace, huge earrings, and megawatt ring to prove it.

"Impossible," he said, looking as if she had said the most ludicrous thing in the world. "In the case of the royal family of Hayat, truly. It is not possible to spend through the riches my family possesses in one lifetime. It is why I am so extravagant with our wealth. Well, that and because it enrages my father to see his money enjoyed by anyone other than him. But what other municipality can boast of having world-class hospitals and entertainment venues with-out having to spend any of their tax revenues? None that I know of. I mean it when I say I will get you a new one."

The revelation of his wealth was slightly breathtaking, even as she knew this pain was about more than simply access to another car. "It was horrible to see it like that."

But rather than indulge her, this time he shrugged and said, "It is just a car."

With a noise of outrage, Rita sat up to look down into his laughing eyes indignantly, saying, "It is not just a car."

Unrepentant, Jag merely rolled his eyes. "Forgive me. It is a one-of-a-kind NECTAR conversion."

Smacking his shoulder, she said, "That's not what I meant."

Sitting up himself, bringing a layer of seriousness to the question, he asked, "What did you mean, then? What is so special about that car that it brought you to tears for the first time in our acquaintance? You left your home and country without a backward glance, and yet a car that is only yours through marriage makes you weep?"

Unprepared for the turn the conversation had taken, Rita paused.

Here was the opportunity to confess, if she were brave enough to do so.

If a night that had included her world debut as NECTAR and as a princess, as well as surviving a sandstorm, had reminded her of anything, it was that she was brave enough to do anything she set her mind to.

She didn't know what Jag would make of her decisions, didn't know if learning just what she had given up in pursuit of her ruined dream would make him look at her in disgust.

But he had shared his secrets with her; it was only fair that she take the same risk with him.

CHAPTER NINE

"When I was seven years old," Rita said, "my father got a commission from a collector to transport his 1962 Ferrari GTO from the Bay Area to Los Angeles. It was already my dream car. I had been ever since I saw one in an episode of *Scooby-Doo* when I was five. When my dad got the order he promised to take me along and he did. We had an amazing time, eating out of gas stations and chatting about cars and the future and electric vehicles. It was so much fun that I promised—to my dad and to myself—that one day I would change the way the world drove, and I would convert a 1962 Ferrari GTO of my very own. My dad laughed at that, pointing out the slim chances of that ever happening."

"Not so slim after all," Jag observed.

Smiling, Rita said softly, "About as slim marrying a prince, I'd say."

"So it is not just a car but a shared dream with your father?" Jag asked.

The innocent assumption chased away Rita's smile.

Shoulders dropping, she shook her head. "No, not a shared dream," she said. "Just mine, it turned out. And one I wanted a little too much in the end."

"How's that?" he asked.

"You mean beyond marrying a stranger to get it?" she asked dryly, proud of how well she echoed his own honed aridity.

Laughing at her, he said, "Yes, beyond that."

Not knowing where to start, Rita drew in a long, slow breath to buy herself a little more time.

Then she opened her mouth and said, "I got into college when I was sixteen years old. My parents were elated. For a moment, I was the pride of my family. But they didn't realize that I had worked so hard and been determined because I wanted to achieve a specific dream, as opposed to being driven to succeed. I wasn't striving to do well because I wanted my family to be proud—honestly, I wasn't even striving for anything at all. I was excelling because I was following a passion that had burned within me from before the time I could talk. I strove because I wanted to impact the world working with the objects that I loved most within it, not because I wanted to impress anyone. Out of that well of passion and conviction, the force and determination behind it, I surprised everyone, not only by graduating early, but by being accepted to a top university."

"You, forceful and determined?" Jag asked, gently teasing.

Closing her eyes, Rita laughed, shaking her head. "I know. It's not shocking. What was shocking, or at least what shocked my father when he found out two years later, was that unbeknownst to him I had not enrolled in the pre-med track that would put me on the path toward becoming an obstetrics and gynecology doctor, but had instead registered as a dual major in mechanical engineering and computer science. He was also rather shocked by the fact that by the time he found out, I was halfway toward completion as well as one of the top students in both programs."

Jag let out an uncharacteristic whistle and Rita couldn't help but smile, even if there was little joy in the expression. Even she was impressed by how bold the story was when she said it out loud.

"I knew I was dealing with a mad genius, but I had no idea she was so titled. I take it that Papa wasn't very pleased when he found out, though?"

Shaking her head, Rita said on an exhale, "Not by a long shot. In fact, he disowned me."

"Excuse me?" Jag asked, utterly serious. "How old were you?"

"Eighteen," Rita said. "A full-fledged adult, in his defense."

"Hardly. And a man who can disown his daughter because she dared to excel in a way he did not approve of needs no defense," Jag said.

Though she hadn't known she needed it, his being defensive on her behalf soothed an old hurt.

Tired, she said, "I deliberately deceived him, and in doing so, stole not just trust and tuition from my family, but also their reputation and my future."

"Explain to me how pursuing your passion stole from your future," he demanded.

Grimacing because they'd come to the shameful and guilt-laden part of the story, Rita said, "When news broke out in our community that I had been accepted to Berkeley at such a young age, it kick-started everything. Families began approaching mine in interest of making matches with their sons, so my family began making arrangements to ensure that I did not miss out on a prosperous future."

"When you were sixteen?" he growled, voice low.

She lifted her palms. "With the caveat that no marriage would take place until I had turned twenty-two. The idea was quite progressive and exciting for the families involved, mine and the one I matched with. My and Rashad's futures would be secure, despite our young ages, while also giving us an opportunity none of our parents had received. We would have the chance to get to know each other, to perhaps fall in love the American way along the process as well."

"And you were fine with all of this?" Jag pressed.

Rita shrugged. "Outside of cars, my family was the most important thing in my world. It didn't seem like a big sacrifice to play the role I was expected to, especially because I didn't understand at first what I was being asked to give up. Rashad was kind and funny and easy to get along with, if a bit distant and aloof. At seventeen, a difference in age of even two years can be a long time, especially with how sheltered and tunnel-visioned I was. But he came from a medical family, which I knew, and the reason they accepted me despite my working-class family, which I did not know, was because of my intelligence, particularly in science and math. With the promise that I would join the medical track, which my father never told me, simply enrolled me and expected me to obey, Rashad's family had offered and my family accepted. In hindsight, it makes sense now why my father took me to register in person. I thought he was proud, but it was really so that he could make sure I was signed up for the right courses. He underestimated my

illfulness, though. He didn't understand that I
vasn't inherently brilliant, but because I loved
ars. And I didn't understand that by going be-
ind his back to change majors and continuing
n with him none the wiser, I had unwittingly
roken my marriage contract, as well as made
ny family look foolish and grasping. My father
lidn't disown me because of what I had done,
hough. He disowned me because when he found
ut and gave me the choice to stop chasing cars
ind behave in a way that put my family first, or
o continue to pursue my dream alone, without
he love, support and warmth of a family and fu-
ure, I chose to walk out the door."

She didn't look at him as she finished her story,
ifraid of the judgment she might see in his ex-
oression, but even fearing that, she felt there was
i weight lifted off her chest in the telling.

Whether or not he thought her selfish, it felt
good to have no dark secrets from him.

"That's no choice," Jag said, his voice heavy
with condemnation, but not of her. Of her father.

"Come again?" Rita asked, startled, having
expected any number of reactions but not protectiveness on her behalf, and in the surprise,
another part of her stitched itself back together.

"What kind of father asks his child to choose
between her dreams and her family? The worst
thing you did wrong was lie in order to do what
you were born to do. Even in deception, you re-

mained a testament to your family. As far as youthful transgressions go," he said with disgust. "I'd say your father got off easy."

"I don't think you understand how poorly my behavior reflected on my family as a whole. If I could be so willful, what did that reflect about my family's values and lessons, about my parents and uncles and sister?"

"I don't think you understand that a real parent's love is dependent not on how their child behaves, but on the miracle that they exist at all. Real love is not conditional, like your family's or my father's, but boundless and unfettered."

"Like your mother's," Rita finished for him softly.

A shadow banked the fires of his eyes, but he did not pull away or deny it. "Like my mother's."

With a soft sigh and smile, Rita said, "What it must have been like to have felt such unconditional love like that."

With no trace of hyperbole, Jag said, "Terrifying," confirming with a single word what Rita had suspected.

"Until the day my father found out," she said, voice still low, "that's what I thought my family felt for me. I never realized that their years of tolerating and indulging my fantasies and dreams had actually been payment in advance for doing my part when the time came."

Taking her hand, he caught her eye to say earnestly, "You made the right choice, Rita. In my experience, conditional love is never truly satisfied, even when its demands are met. It will simply demand more and more until failure is guaranteed because conditional love is not about love at all, but power. If you had sacrificed the things that made you *you*, they would have only asked for more. Instead, here you are, better to yourself and the world than you ever would have been had you allowed them to clip your wings."

It took a moment for his words to penetrate, as if they had to travel through thick layers of calluses left by years of hard feelings between her and her father.

But as they did, something broke open inside her, a box filled with grief, and guilt, and shame—all of the feelings that she had carried and shoved deep down inside in order to survive the pain of separation and loneliness of being cast out from her family.

All of the self-doubt and second-guessing that she had taken on as her responsibility and used to create a hard protective shell started to crack and crumble and fall apart like the ruin she and the Prince sat atop.

For the third time that night, Rita's eyes welled up with tears, this set years overdue.

Unlike those she'd cried for the car, these were silent tears, racking her body with force that felt like it could tear her apart.

Like before, Jag's arm came around her, draw ing her into the warm circle of his embrace, this time all the more comforting for the heat that radiated upward from the stone they sat upon.

Rocking her, he made soothing sounds, like a mother.

The experience was so unexpected that it took Rita a moment to realize, between heaving gasps and big wet tears, that the shooshing noises were not coming from the wind, but from him.

"Shh. Shh. Shhh. There, there," he murmured voice a low rumble against her form.

She didn't know when she had crawled into his lap, but at some point in the process of envel oping herself in the arms he'd offered, she had.

Giving in fully, she nestled her head in the crook of his neck and closed her eyes, letting the warmth and comfort he provided seep through her suit and ease the ache of being alone all these years.

He held her there, quietly rocking her back and forth, for a long time.

Long enough that her body stilled, calming in its silent hyperventilating, and her tears ebbed and dried.

Long enough that other inputs began process ing—his bare skin, the smell of him on her and all around her, the feeling of being wrapped in the safety of his strength.

She slowed her breathing so that she could savor every warm strong inhale of him.

He stilled further at her movement, his own breath going shallow as hers went deeper.

Wrung out, not even a lifetime of lessons and inhibitions were enough to overcome the powerful tide rising in her now. She had shown him her full self, and he had affirmed her right to be and think and feel just the way she was.

Like love, he made demands of her, but unlike love, when he pushed her, it was into bravery, into being more fully and authentically herself. He wasn't trying to mold her; instead he affirmed time and time again that he wanted her because of exactly who she was.

And if he'd affirmed that what they'd told her about love might be wrong, could he not do the same for sex?

If love did not always have to coerce and demand, then perhaps sex didn't either. Perhaps it was possible to be two people committed to caring for each other, enjoying each other's bodies. Perhaps it was okay to simply feel good.

Wrapping her arms around his waist, pressing her face deeper into his neck, she squeezed.

Above her, he groaned, the sound like something in him giving up, and his arms closed fully around her, trapping her now whereas before he had merely held the space for her—as if he held something precious.

Twisting in his arms, she rearranged her body, maneuvering into a new position in order to assuage the urge that demanded she get closer still. Straddling him, lifting her arms up to wrap around his neck where her fingers could dive into his thick, silky hair.

He did not squander the opportunity that their new position offered, either, tightening his hold on her so that her breasts pressed against his chest and her core against the rigid hardness at the apex of his thighs, ushering in a rush of liquid heat at her center.

He brought one arm up the middle of her back to cup her skull and slowly tilt her face toward the sky, gently exposing the column of her neck.

When his lips pressed against the tender, delicate skin there, a fireworks explosion of sensations went off inside her.

Never before had another person's lips touched her in such a way, and she marveled at the pliable pressure that masked the insistent demand of his mouth against her.

Here and there, his tongue darted out, taking tiny tastes of her, leaving her tingling and breathless.

He kissed her shoulders and collarbone through her suit, drawing her attention to those and countless other sensitive places she'd never been aware of.

Working his way up her neck, he left a trail of

stirring kisses, soft warm breaths, and teasing bursts of cool air pushed out through pursed lips.

When he reached her jawline, his hands joined in the action, trailing up the sides of her body to cup her face, cradling it as he placed long, soft kisses at the outside corners of each of her eyes, her temples and earlobes before coming back to kiss the spot between her eyebrows with the same deliberate tenderness.

Pulling back only slightly, he caught Rita in the mesmerizing fire that was his gaze once more. "Do you want me, Rita?" he asked, tension in every word.

"Like I have never wanted another," Rita breathed.

His pupils dilated at her words, understanding what she said beneath them—it was what she had meant when she'd told him that she was from an old-fashioned family before, that she had never been intimate with anyone else—and then he was kissing her, their lips meeting in a dance older than the ruins they sat upon.

She hadn't known what she expected him to taste like, but it hadn't been honey and cardamom, a sweet thickness she could gladly lose herself in.

Nipping his bottom lip, there was no timidity in her exploration of her prince.

When she ran her fingers down his neck, scratching the bare skin of his shoulders and trailing down his back, he groaned, pulling her closer and pressing her hips to grind against the hard shaft of his erection.

The tender, sensitive buds of her nipples hardened further, raking against his bare chest, the only thing separating them the thin high-tech material of her clothing, which was barely a separation at all.

And at the same time, it was unbearable.

Her body cried for the freedom to feel, skin to skin, the hands that caressed her up and down, that gripped her bottom and spread her thighs to press her molten core closer against the hard plane of his abs.

Suddenly, she was bitter for the excellent quality of her clothing.

If it had not been sealed so well she would already be as bare as her husband, already have achieved the further closeness her body knew was possible and strained for.

With a dry laugh, Jag whispered in her ear, voice strained, "Slow down, my sweet, sweet wife, this is no race. I've imagined savoring you like this, like the NECTAR you so aptly named yourself, so many times, I would be shameful to rush."

His words, their deep rumble yet another form of sensual simulation, traveled the lines of her body like rivers of lava heating and stirring in their carnal promise.

Rita had waited long enough, though.

She had waited twenty-seven years to be accepted and adored as she was now, with reverence rather than the intent to mold.

Hands growing bolder, Rita explored Jag's body freely, trailing over the sculpted shoulders and arms, squeezing, scratching, lingering and digging in as she pleased to the intoxicating chorus of the sounds of his pleasure.

His tongue probed deeper, hands to her breasts, his thumbs caressing her hardened nipples once more. The dual attack split her focus, splintering and captivating the forces that had only moments before been intent on conquest.

Her breasts, high and tight and fully alert, trembled beneath the onslaught of his attention, and the sensation threatened to carry her away, though into what she had no idea.

Crying out, she gripped him tight as he tortured her through the thin barrier of her clothing. She could not have stopped the moans of pleasure coming from her if she had wanted to and as it was, she didn't want to. In this moment, the only thing that existed was her and him in the vast expanse of empty night desert around them. She could be as loud as she wanted to.

"It's time to get you out of these clothes," he said, an implacable chord of certainty woven throughout his voice like rebar.

And she agreed.

With more patience than she would have been able to manage, he reached up behind her neck to release the clasp that held the heavy chandelier necklace in place.

Setting it to the side gently, he went for the belt next, his hands lingering on the outer edges of her thighs and trailing up to cup her bottom and squeeze, before rounding the curve to remove the belt of astounding pearls.

Next, placing his palms on her shoulders, he trailed his hands down her arms, gently slipping her bracelets off when coming to them in his unhurried caress.

He then took her left hand, turning her palm upright, gently spinning the ring into the center of her hand and folding her fingers over it so the mighty rock lay safely tucked in the palm of her hand. Then his hands came back to her neck, finding the hidden zipper that blended near seamlessly into the line of her catsuit.

Staring deep into her eyes, he began to pull down the zipper, gently peeling the fitted material down, exposing the bare skin of her shoulders, then her sternum, pausing only after releasing the large soft globes of her breasts.

Eyes smoldering, he told her everything she needed to know about his reaction to what he saw with the heat in his gaze.

But as if sensing how far an affirmation

would go, he said, "Even more beautiful than I imagined."

Heat flushed Rita's skin, a dusky blush deepening the brown tone everywhere that it was visible.

Licking his lips, Jag returned to her true unveiling.

Though this was the first time any adult had ever seen her naked body, Rita felt entirely comfortable.

More than comfortable. Powerful.

The man before her might be a world leader capable of commanding the respect of the international community, but in this he was helpless to his desire for her.

She held the key—was the answer—to the only thing he wanted.

Only she could give it to him. Only he could give it to her.

And then she was as naked as he was, but for the enormous ring on her left hand that sparkled in the moonlight.

Bared to her husband for the first time, no barriers between them, she was filled with a sense of virtue. They might not have entered marriage this way, but here, finally, they came together for the right reasons.

His eyes consumed her, raking over her form, leaving invisible marks of their possession in their fiery trail.

He swallowed, the sound audible to them both in the hyper-focused bubble that had grown up to encircle them.

Clearing his throat, he said, his words thick and rough, "You are perfection."

And seeing it in his eyes, she believed him.

CHAPTER TEN

RITA IN THE moonlight was beauty incarnate. Blessed with a shockingly hourglass figure— shocking because perfect symmetry was rare in nature and yet abundant in her—Rita's breasts were buoyant and full, exactly the size and density necessary to really counterbalance the glorious round peach of her hips and bottom.

Her legs were proportionally long and shapely, her feet adorable, with red-painted toenails.

The cinch of her waist emphasized the balance of top and bottom, while her stomach was an expression of smooth slopes rather than cut definition—just the way he liked it.

By everything that was good and holy, she was sex on wheels.

Jag's palms itched, ready to be all over her once more, this time unimpeded by the barrier of her clothing.

He wanted to trail hot kisses down her stomach and beyond.

He wanted her from the front, from behind,

and on top of him—riding him, holding him in the vise grip of her strong thighs—all at once.

Guiding her to lie, he rose above her, taking in her satiny expanse of brown skin and the way her dark hair feathered around her. Her eyes were huge black pits in the moonlight fixed upon him. She would follow where he led, and he did not take it for granted. Not with this woman, whose ferocious independence had given her the courage to strike out on her own in a world not made for her. And she had made it, had proved to herself and the world that she needed no man to lead her.

But here she was willing to follow, trusting he would take them through the labyrinthine halls of pleasure to both of their benefits. Suddenly grateful for his lifetime of dissolute practice.

Lowering himself over her, he brought his lips to hers in yet another long, lingering kiss. Despite the driving urge to possess her, he'd meant what he said to her earlier. As much as he knew this woman loved speed, what happened tonight between them would be no race.

Trailing kisses from her lips down her throat and over between the valley of her breasts, he began his southward journey, reveling in the out-of-this-world softness of her skin with every press of his lips.

Underneath the blanket of his attention, she writhed and moaned, her hands taking on a mind of their own as her control dissipated in wave after wave of sensation.

Could he thank her without words? Could he send her body into the throes of ecstasy in repayment for the dark and twisted game she had agreed to play with him? Could he repay her for her perfection, her capacity to meet each of his demands and still have more to give?

He could.

Rita was a revelation. Her skin as smooth as satin, its scent reminiscent of the heavy sweetness of night blooms, she beckoned him to touch, caress and taste.

And so he did.

Savoring her textures, he kissed his way down her body. But he did not make a beeline for the heated center of her. There was so much to explore before.

He licked and kissed and nibbled a path, leaving a trail of his marks.

He rubbed his beard along the sensitive skin of her inner thighs and she shivered, as responsive to his touch as the vehicles she created.

Had he ever had a lover who was so attuned to everything he did?

She was a woman of eagle-eyed focus, and now all of it was tuned in to the things he did to her. Had he ever had this power?

He had been born a prince. In the desert moonlight, she made him a god.

Trailing his fingertips from the arch of her foot up her inner thigh, he pressed a hot palm against the silky expanse of her skin, gently opening her thighs and exposing her further. She sucked a breath in when the night air touched her most intimate seam, and he had to take a slow breath himself in order not to plunder what lay before him.

He had promised them slow, even if her hips moved in a way that was nothing if not an invitation to dive in. She didn't know what she stood to miss in a race to the finish line—he owed it to her to show her.

While continuing his oral adoration of her thighs, her brought one palm up to cup her mound, holding her there, his steady grip firm, hot and gentle, and her sensitized sex opened further, its liquid heat evidence of her growing readiness.

He began to undulate his fingers in slow waves with gentle pressure against the sensitive bud at her center, confident the steady, slow motion would take her exactly where he wanted her.

She arched her lower back on a long moan before falling back again with a shiver.

He could not have dreamed up a more responsive lover. Would never dream of another.

Where he cupped her, her deepest layers pulled at him, their slick invitation an irresistible siren call. Deviating from his intention, if only slightly, he pressed the heel of his hand against her core.

Bucking in response, she shuddered out a hiss of a breath, and he smiled again.

She was ready for him now, her body eager to welcome him in its slick, wet embrace—but they still had so much to explore.

When her moans rang out across the desert to the beat of his heart, he kept up the motion with an even speed and pace until she was left panting and whimpering, her fingers reaching for him desperately, seeking his skin to grip and hold.

It took all he had not to be greedy with his gift, to gobble her all up in an instant.

He had at least taken his time enough to have earned a taste. The reasoning drew him toward her center, had him kissing the core of her.

If her flavor had hinted at sweet blooms before, she was a full bouquet now, thick and syrupy and celestial. It was not enough to taste, he had to feast—and so he did.

She cried out his name, her hand finding a hold in his hair, and the sound drove him on, urging him to take more ground, and faster, like the most relentless charioteer.

To draw it out for her, he resisted, held back the will whose every whim was the status quo. A prince got what he wanted. A man could bow to her needs.

He tasted her steadily, lapping at her core until

she was trembling and moaning and teetering on the edge of collapse.

Bringing his fingers to join his mouth, he traced the edges of her while devouring her, and she screamed, body going rigid for an instant before she curved around him, her thighs tightening around his head in an intimate clinch.

She remained locked around him like that for the sweetest eternity before collapsing back against the still-warm stones, temporarily gone to the world, undone by her orgasm.

A moment later, because she had been blessed to be born in the form of a glorious woman, her eyes opened, luminescent, and she smiled, the expression brighter than the moon.

Reaching toward him, she pulled him up to wrap her arms around his neck and bury her face against him, nuzzling and squeezing, her legs simultaneously curling around to hold him as if it were not enough to hold him in the embrace of just her arms. It was intoxicatingly sweet.

Without guile, she angled her body into the exact position necessary for his access, her body a beacon that his was instinctively driven to seek out, and his muscles strained while he continued to hold himself back.

There was no going back from this point; the knowledge was a truth in him as certain as his need to venture forth anyway. The last of his will faltering in the face of the heat that radiated from her, he knew he was lost.

The tip of his erection pressed along the hot core of her, and he paused.

Her focus, too, was zeroed in on the place where their bodies touched.

"I—" The word came out rough and unwelcome in the face of the perfection of this moment. "I don't have a condom," he finished. He hated the words for being true, himself for being unprepared on the most important night of his life. As attuned to her emotion as he was now, however, he wouldn't take what was not clearly given.

Irritation—primal and fast and the most merciful sight he had ever seen—flashed across her eyes. But he did not move until she spoke.

"I don't care. Don't stop. You can't stop now," she demanded.

Immense relief washed through his system to mingle with everything else she stirred up. She was strategic and thoughtful. She would not be cavalier if pregnancy was a possibility.

Most important to him in this moment, however, was that she did not want him to stop.

Mindful of her inexperience, he eased in gently, he entered her, slowly and steadily relying on the controlled application of his weight for pressure, giving her body time to open and adjust to his intrusion, even as the viselike grip of her undulated and pulsed around him, dragging him close to climax faster than any self-respecting lover would admit to.

Not even during his first time had the simple act of sliding inside a woman brought him so close to the precipice.

Ever the rebel, Rita blew away what he'd thought sex was, redefining the act into something more intimate and dangerous than he had ever experienced.

His muscles strained, torn by the barrage of his conflicting needs. He needed to please her, he needed to fully sheathe himself within her, he needed to break away from her, to run before the tendrils of emotions that floated between them hooked into him and never let go.

Beneath him, she moaned, and the sound curled around him, as much of a trap as the way their bodies joined, fitting together like two pieces of the most complicated human puzzle.

And when their bodies clenched and his shaft was fully encased within her, he lost his breath, his sight momentarily replaced by flashes of light, like the twinkle of stars in the night sky, and the only thing that held him back from shaming himself was his commitment to make her come again.

After two long, slow strokes, he knew they could not continue this way, not with her breasts grazing his chest, her inner thighs caressing his flanks, and the dark wells of her eyes, incandescent and mesmerizing in the moonlight, staring up at him. She wanted him to release his ultimate core of control and give it all to her, to let himself crack open in her presence. She didn't ask for it in words, but with her body. Her energy seducing it from him, promising that it wouldn't hurt to be vulnerable with her, that it would feel sinfully good.

Unable to take it, he drew her up, maintaining his steady, impossibly sweet stroke as he repositioned her, bearing the bulk of the weight of her pleasure-limp form until he finally had to reluctantly withdraw in order to guide her onto her hands and knees.

He would not embarrass himself if he could no longer see her pleasure in her eyes, if her breasts did not brush against him each time their hips met. He told himself the lie even as the new vision she presented him threatened him as well.

But if he didn't let it wash over him, the primal urge from seeing her perfectly round behind in the air, her hips waiting for his grip, he would be fine.

In his calculations, however, he didn't account for the intimate physics of human joining, hadn't recalled that when he slid into her from behind, he would not find space but even more profound joining. He had forgotten in his drive for distance that the position would only carry him deeper.

But still he held back, biding his time, patient

without grace, as he stoked up the growing tension in her body again, building her to a crescendo once more, edging her closer and closer to another collapse.

Nearing the point where he could either continue to see to his woman and lose himself or direct all of his focus to holding back, he released one hip with a caress of farewell before reaching his hand around her to once again cup her mound. The move drew her closer, tucked her body tighter in the protective arch of his own as his thumb found the sensitive bud at the apex of her opening, bringing a tendril of tenderness to their tireless dance that sweetened and thickened the joining, even as he sought to bring them both the escape of climax.

They could not get closer, he reasoned, if they both fell apart.

But the increased sweetness between them only deepened the pleasure of the experience. Rita reveled in it, arching her back and crying out, unconsciously deepening his access as she shattered around him again. Her inner muscles spasmed in powerful waves, the pull and tug of them drawing him further still. A surge of final need thickened his shaft within her, locking him in place as he spiraled toward the inevitable and impending death of everything that he had been before her.

His climax destroyed him, as if his sole purpose in life—the very reason he had been put on this planet—had been to give her this moment. To love her.

And because his body, still pulsing with tremors of pleasure, still beating and throbbing inside hers, wanted only to ease further into her, he did not pull her close to hold and cushion her comedown.

He couldn't, not when his own protective barriers were down, his system rocked as it never had been before. He was exposed to her in this moment, as vulnerable as the sanded Ferrari because he could not separate the one-of-a-kind experience he'd just had with her from the her herself.

Neither did he allow himself the reprieve of falling back against the warm stone to breath deep and look at the stars overhead while she snuggled in beside him, as his instincts urged him to do.

Instead, he painstakingly withdrew from her, gentle even as he was thorough in his distancing. Their bodies resisted separation, held on to each other like lovers lingering at a train station.

Her small sound of protest at his leaving pierced his chest, but as the transcendent bliss of having her cooled, it was replaced with resolved contrition.

He had had her once, and he could never risk it again. Not when just a single taste tempted him to stop fighting, to let down the barriers, reveal everything he held within inside and give her the power to compel him—to twist him to her will.

And if not her, then anyone who wanted to get to him through her.

In having her, he had created that doorway. There was no way things would go back to being as simple and smooth as they had been up to now.

He should never have brought her here in the first place.

He should have heeded Rafael's advice and taken greater strides to avoid being alone with her.

Obviously, it was too late for that wisdom now; and *shoulds* and *oughts* were a weak man's nostalgia. The breach had already occurred, but the damage could yet be controlled. He simply need not do it again. Now that he had tasted the ambrosia of NECTAR, now that he knew that she held within her a wellspring of the sweetest elixir, however, the task would be easier said than done.

It was saying something when losing a priceless Ferrari to a sandstorm was the least of an action's consequences.

Constructing an invisible wall between them, he reached for her hand and kissed the back of it, smiling a smile that did not reach his eyes, and said, "I'm afraid that our stone heater here is running out of fuel, so it's time to bring our lovely little party to a close."

Eyes wide, filled with confusion that battled hurt, she stammered, "O-okay."

He felt her baffled sting as if it were his own, but could not allow the situation to go any further. It was better for both of them that this fire be doused now—and thoroughly.

The success of their partnership depended upon them not developing feelings for each other. They could never get close enough that they introduced the opportunity for betrayal. Acquaintances could not hurt each other. Could not be used against each other.

Looking away from her, freeing himself from the shame, and sting of her bewilderment, he reached for the phone that lay cold on the warm stone. He dialed quickly, calling their pickup and a change of clothes with efficiency that only highlighted how foolish and unnecessary a risk his little excursion had been. He should never have broken the seal, neither of her innocence nor on his ignorance of what it would be like to be inside her.

He had made love to his wife when it had been entirely avoidable, and now, inevitably, given the nature of their situation, nothing would ever be the same.

CHAPTER ELEVEN

Despite being possessed of a mind powerful enough to send her to Berkeley at sixteen and to create some of the world's most innovative vehicles, postcoital etiquette was an area in which she had no basis of knowledge.

For example, she had no idea if it was normal to feel not pain or awkwardness or shock in her body, but a relaxed liquid joy, as if the muscle of her happiness had flexed to its utmost tension before letting go with a sigh.

She wanted to curl into Jag, not to go another round—though a giggly part of her insisted that wasn't a bad idea—but because she wanted to bathe in his scent and fall asleep in his arms.

He, on the other hand, seemed more interested in getting them home.

Maybe he was tired? Maybe he was just depleted now and eager to get to his bed.

She wouldn't mind a glass of water herself, and while they weren't helpless, they were currently stranded in the desert.

But a part of her protested the idea.

If it was considered rude to use one's phone at the dinner table, it seemed like the rule would apply the moments following an experience like the one she had just shared with Jag.

Never in her wildest dreams had she ever imagined that sex would be anything like what had just happened between them.

No wonder the world was obsessed.

No wonder Jag had been so certain it would change things between them.

Rita didn't think it was possible to open oneself to another human being the way that they each had just done and have things remain static between them—but after her night with him she no longer agreed that it couldn't be done.

Remaining strangers couldn't be done, but that wasn't because they'd had sex. It was because over the course of the past weeks, they'd become friends.

They could see their arrangement through simply because they cared about supporting each other.

If anything, she was more sure of that now than she had been before.

In fact, watching Jag, the only thing she could even think of to change was the comedown, and even on that front was willing to accept that there were drawbacks to outside in the moonlight.

Wrapping up his conversation, Jag hung up

the phone before saying to Rita, "Our ride will arrive shortly. We should make our way back to the car and the road—the time it will take us to get there should mean our path and the driver's will converge upon arrival."

His tone was all business and clipped, nothing like the way he'd been talking to her since they'd left the exhibition, nor even over the past weeks. Resisting the urge to frown, she told herself it was a sign he had realized the same thing.

However, after his next words she began to wonder that they had not come to exactly the same place.

The administrative clip in his voice confirmed her suspicions when he said, "Don't forget your bracelets. I set them just there," he said, pointing to the small pile of precious jewels beside her jacket, before adding, "and about tonight…" He paused, as if he searched for the words and they did not come easily. But then he confused her even more, with his next words. "In the interest of keeping things simple, I suggest we put this little incident behind us and return to business as usual, moving forward."

While she had been thinking in a similar vein, her train of thought had contained some very critical differences, including the character and nature of what they had shared.

Was he serious? Business as usual? It seemed

pretty clear to Rita that that wasn't one of the options on their table.

But it was clear he thought it was, and not knowing what else to do, she simply nodded.

There was no route by which she could return to the way things had been before, but if he thought that meant they must be even more vigilant that it should never happen again, then she couldn't coerce him.

Instead, she said, "Sure," lightly, matching his energy.

He said nothing to her anemic reply, and she took his silence as a reprieve from the effort of pretending to be less affected than she was.

With wobbly hands, she tugged the zipper of her suit, snagging it when she came to the collar seam at the base of her neck.

"Let me help," he said, his warm fingers replacing her rapidly chilling ones to clasp the tiny metal tag. His hands lingered on her neck, warm and tender, before leaving with a light caress, its faint touch so soft it could have been accidental.

Then he stepped away from her once more, and the coldness rushed back in to surround them again.

Though she had been coming to feel like she was learning to read him, she could not understand him now.

Rather than his usual firm and efficient, his actions now appeared brittle and edgy, and yet outwardly he merely ensured they would make it home before daylight.

When she was dressed once more, they made their way back down the crumbling staircase to the desert floor, and from there they walked quietly back to the wrecked vehicle they had abandoned earlier.

As he had predicted, their driver awaited their arrival in a sleek black town car.

Once he saw them, the driver stepped out holding in his hands a bundle of folded clothing.

Taking the clothes from the man, Jag walked around the other side of the car and clothed himself while Rita entered the back seat through the door the driver had opened for her.

Moments later, Jag joined her, sliding into the seat, his attention focused on the phone in his hand.

They spent the rest of the drive that way, Jag engrossed in his device, Rita staring at the night outside, her mind wrapped up in wondering how long they were going to pretend their arrangement could go on as it had before.

CHAPTER TWELVE

EIGHT WEEKS LATER, Rita was no closer to an answer, and had, in fact, only driven herself sick in dwelling on it. The most obvious reason—that she'd become pregnant from her night with Jag—had already been ruled out by the particularly emotional period that had followed it, just days later.

She was utterly exhausted and could not remember the last time she had made it through an entire night without her bladder waking her at least once to use the restroom.

Her skin, too, seemed affected, becoming sensitive and tender as if now that she had had sex once, she should experience actual pain from the lack of it.

Maintaining the line Jag had reestablished for them even as the ashes of it still burned from how thoroughly they had set it aflame, they had not had sex again.

In fact, she hadn't really seen Jag since.

It appeared that their intimacy had had opposite effects on each of them, even if it came to the same conclusion: deeper commitment to maintaining their agreement.

And now she had lost her appetite and could no longer reliably keep down even the scant food she felt like eating.

Losing weight as a result, she could suddenly understand what people meant when they said they were wasting away.

She found herself spending long stretches of time, sometimes entire days, replaying the night of the debut and what had happened afterward in her mind, trying to figure out how a man could go from making her the center of his attention to behaving as if she were an acquaintance in the blink of an eye.

True to his word, Jag had indeed endeavored to keep things professional between them, no longer coming home for dinner most nights, and scheduling a three-week trip abroad, leaving Rita in Hayat.

Now that she was publicly his wife, and gaining her own popularity with car-loving citizens, he had told her before departing, with her security detail, she would be safe enough from his father that Jag believed they could reasonably afford the risk of the trip.

Or so he said.

With all of that time to herself to think, Rita

nad come up with other theories, as well as more questions.

Mulling over it all once again, however, she meandered into the blue dining room to have yet another meal alone.

Walking into the room, she was welcomed by a bouquet of aromas.

Rafida had set the table already, including the cinnamon porridge she knew Rita loved, fresh fruit, dates, and yogurt with honey. There were fragrant flowers, as always, and freshly squeezed orange juice. It all looked beautiful—and Rita got one whiff of it and dropped to her hands and knees, gagging, as dry heaves overtook her.

Rafida walked in carrying a tray of bread and, seeing Rita, dropped it with a clatter and ran over. She placed her hands on Rita's cheeks and forehead before bringing them to rest on Rita's shoulders as she guided Rita back out of the room and into the cooler, less aromatic hallway.

Moments later, Rita was more settled, her wave of nausea having passed. After propping Rita against the wall, Rafida hurried off to retrieve something for her to drink.

Rita had expected a glass of ice water, but Rafida came back with a mug filled with what looked like hot water.

"Here, have a sip of this," she said.

Trusting, Rita took a drink and nearly spit it

out. Inside was not just warm water, but vinegar and, if she wasn't mistaken, sugar.

The combination of strong yet nonspecific flavors was an attack on her senses—until it wasn't.

As the sip settled, so too did her stomach—her whole system, really.

The strange concoction had done the job, and Rita was grateful.

Gingerly, she rose to her feet, Rafida hovering nearby to offer a hand of support if she needed.

Smiling and mildly embarrassed, Rita said, "Thank you, Rafida. I'm glad you were there. I don't know what came over me, but your vinegar drink has cured me."

She turned back toward the dining room as she spoke, prepared to return to the beautiful breakfast that Rafida had laid out for her, when the older woman reached out to take her hand and stop her.

"I don't think you want to go back in there, Princess."

Frowning at the title—she'd tried to get Rafida to stop calling her that—Rita said, "Of course I do. Whatever is going on with me is my problem, not breakfast's. Your food looks delicious as ever."

A smile growing on her face, Rafida shook her head. "Not a problem, a pregnancy. I'm no doctor, but I'm certain when I say that you're going to have a baby."

For a moment nothing processed. Rita didn't breathe. No thoughts crossed her mind. No maternal warnings, voices or images rushed in to guide or provide understanding.

Just a moment of utter blankness.

But like the disappearance of the shoreline before a tsunami, the silence was no reprieve but a dire warning of the wave to come.

There came a rumbling and roaring in her veins and ears, the sound of the abrupt transforming of the very landscape of her life.

Thoughts whipped around in her mind like whirlwinds, further churning the already-roiling incoming tide.

Her husband had gotten her pregnant.

At her side, Rafida beamed, her reaction the standard and congratulatory joy for an expecting newly married couple.

Like nails on a chalkboard, it raked against Rita's nerves.

She and Jag were not a joyfully married young couple.

Rafida has to be aware of that, Rita thought crossly. She saw them interact—or *not*, rather.

There was no way she could be as deeply embedded into their household as she was and not know that it was purely business beneath their romantic facade.

Her husband's absolute lack of meaningful

feeling toward her had to be obvious for anyone who had eyes to see.

And this was the same man she was going to have a child with.

That she was married to.

She had given up her anonymity and her country for the chance to change the world but instead she wound up pregnant, abroad and alone.

And she didn't even know where her husband was.

She was thousands of miles away from her home base and now she had become responsible for another being's life—a being whose father had already made it clear that he didn't want things getting awkward between them.

With the emerging development of her pregnancy, there was no way to prevent things from getting extremely awkward.

They were going to have a baby.

CHAPTER THIRTEEN

IT WAS 2:00 A.M. when Jag returned to the palace, walking the halls quietly on his way to the room that was his to sleep in had he ever decided to.

In the two months that had passed since he'd made love to Rita, he had become such an expert at keeping busy that he had finally hit a wall in which he had nothing more to do. Pregnancy was not his concern—she would have surely cared about a condom had that been a possibility—but the experience nonetheless harried his every spare minute as if he were a young man worried about getting a girl in a bad situation. He'd used that energy to drive his recent efficiency until that well ran dry, too.

Considering all of the follow-up necessary for an event as large as the exhibition, and everything that was needed to take down a corrupt king, he should have felt triumphant.

Instead, it had only further complicated matters.

He had nothing left to distract himself with.

And with nothing left to distract him, his mind invariably returned to Rita.

And tonight, he returned in person. But only to sleep beneath the same roof. He would not sleep with her again. He had tasted her forbidden fruit once and was already struggling with withdrawals. Twice and he would surely go past the point of no return.

But he could be near her. He had nothing left strong enough to keep him away.

His popularity had skyrocketed. International interest and tourism spiking, with Rita's name at the center. And Jag was the most popular living monarch Hayat had ever seen—and he wasn't even reigning.

And because of it, the press conference in which he would reveal and condemn his father had been scheduled.

He had had a personal hand in planning every element of the event. It would be perfect. But now all there was to do was sit back and wait for the big day.

And though he expected more to come in, he had finally made his way through the backlog of international trade offers and shiny new contracts that had been on his desk after the exhibition.

Now there was nothing else to keep him away from Rita.

So he had come home.

Was it home because it was the only place he

had spent happy years, or was it because she was here?

He hated himself for asking the question.

Since Rita had arrived, even when he dined with her, he had been so good about leaving for whatever residence was nearest with traffic at the time. It didn't matter; he was only going to toss and turn dreaming about Rita anyway.

And that had been before he was inside her.

But tonight, as weak as his will had become—or more likely because of it—there was nothing that would stop him from at least sleeping in the same building as her.

This was how he broke.

This was how he drove himself to the only place he'd ever called home, uninterested in a driver or witness for the trip, staring out at the long stretch of desert beyond the city and seeing Rita.

Slipping into the room that was his. Or would be if he ever spent the night here.

Closing his eyes as he passed through the doorway, he could almost smell her, his mind supplying the details. Her scent reached out of his memory to wrap around him like the climbing and clinging vines of the sweet night-blooming jasmine that she always brought to his mind.

Then he realized that though the room was darkened, he wasn't alone.

His memory had not supplied her scent in such

vivid detail that his nose could not tell the difference between imagination and reality, but rather her living and breathing self had in his bed.

He had set her up in a different wing when he'd installed her in the palace. It appeared things had changed in his absence.

He wished the observation did not make the corners of his mouth want to lift.

"I know you're here, Jag," she said by way of greeting, her body still and back to him as she lay on her side.

"How did you know it was me?" he asked quietly.

"I could smell you," she said.

Frowning, he said, "My apologies. I didn't mean to come into your room. I thought you were in the guest wing."

Rolling around to face him, her expression still shadowed in the dark room, she said, "Rafida moved my things here as soon as she heard the news."

Jag bowed his head to the absurd logic of it. Of course; he had not anticipated it, but it made sense nonetheless.

And because of it, not only did he find himself beneath the same roof as the woman he desperately needed to get off his mind, but in the same bedroom.

He needed to get out.

Clearing his throat, he said, "In that case,

'm sorry for disturbing your rest. I'll let you get back to it." He began to step out, pulling the door closed as he spoke, knowing he shouldn't even be in here.

"Jag, stop." Her voice was a command, and he stopped.

He pushed the door back open with a creak, though never in his life had he ever recalled a palace door creaking.

He stood silhouetted in the door because as low and gentle as the hall lighting was, it was still brighter than the dark of the bedroom.

The dark from which Rita's disembodied voice emerged to say, "I'm pregnant."

He had been worried about the wrong threat all this time. He had been worried that the tendrils of warmth and homecoming he felt when he was around her, the threads of connection that had only grown, exponentially, since he'd made love to her, were the thing to watch out for.

But no. It was the one that should have been the most obvious from the beginning.

He was no different from Vin, nor Rafael, nor Zeus.

Undone by the oldest side effect in the known universe.

Rita was pregnant.

She had obviously become so the night they made love in the desert. The timing and the circumstances made sense, after all.

She had never been with anyone else. They had not used a condom, could not have, as in his undress he'd been in the rare state of not having one. There you had it.

As a healthy modern male, he maintained excellent sexual health, getting the appropriate tests and checkups regularly enough to ensure that he posed no risk to the partners he took, and still, he was typically very careful to ensure that he was protected in return.

Making love to Rita had been the most transcendent experience of his life, and one that he had been patently reckless regarding the possible consequences of.

But for this to happen.

He was undone. And what about his plans? Should he change them now, the risk of unrest not just a matter of the comfort of his people but the safety of his child?

This was almost to a T the exact situation he had taken such great pains to avoid.

To have things unravel at the end like this, because of this, was just so, so primitive. For it to have come down to a condom was so damn *old-fashioned*.

"You're not on the pill? You said you didn't care about a condom. What does that mean, if not that contraception is taken care of?" he asked, his tone sharper than he had a right to, unthinking to the fact that those would be the first words he would say in response to the first time he found out about his impending fatherhood for eternity.

He could think about that later.

Right now he wanted to know why the woman who created the world's leading electric vehicles and was passionate about the future and technology and machines was not on the pill.

She was all that was modern and liberated from natural cycles. Shouldn't she be on the pill?

"Excuse me?" Rita asked, outrage lifting the volume of her voice.

Belatedly, Jag realized that she had likely played out a number of scenarios in preparing to deliver the news to him. She had likely feared his reaction and worried that he would be angry with her, and the edge in his voice and immediate interrogation were not likely to be dissuading her from those notions.

But he couldn't seem to find the control he was famous for to do anything about it.

He was angry.

But not at her.

He was angry at himself. How could he have let this happen? Because far more fairly than his words implied, he knew it had been his fault. He should have had greater self-control. He should have resisted.

None of that, however, stopped him from digging his hole deeper. "The pill," he repeated. "Aren't you on it? Aren't all women on the pill these days?" he grumbled, recognizing that the answer was obvious.

Lifting to her elbow, she cocked her head to the side and lifted an eyebrow. "Are you done?"

Sighing, he closed his eyes and answered his own question. "Obviously the answer is no. If you'd been on the pill, you would not be pregnant." He was being an ass. He was being an ass because if there was any fault to be had, it was primarily his own. He had let desire drive away logic, assuming far more than she'd ever implied. A man in his position knew far, far better than that. Opening them again, he said, "I'm sorry, Rita."

Only now did he realize she wore an ice-blue silk nightgown beneath the sheet that draped over her hips, hugged her curves, while the gown framed her cleavage.

Only now, his eyes adjusted to the dark and his life no longer his own, was he able to take note of her breasts, and how their increased size already hinted at her pregnancy.

Stepping back into the room, his nostrils flaring to catch the scent of her, he remained in control of his voice at least, when he said, "I should have never assumed."

How could he have been so reckless?

Rita was pregnant.

The world's most remarkable, beautiful and ingenious woman was going to have his baby.

He went to the bed, kneeling to take her hand, which remained stiff between his palms until he repeated, "I'm sorry, Rita. None of that is what I meant to say. I was a fool. What I meant to ask was how are you feeling?"

And then she melted into him, her lush body pliable and lovely in his arms. "Sick, but Rafida assures me that it's a sign the baby is healthy."

Breathing into her hair, he closed his eyes as the wave of realization swept over him.

He had a child to protect.

"Rafida would know."

For the third time since he had met her, Rita split him in half. There was a Jag that had existed before this moment, and a Jag that existed now.

The first time had been when she became his wife.

The second, when he made love to her in the moonlight.

And now, the third, as she made him a father.

Their agreement was shot.

There would no longer be an end date on their contract—they would share a child for the rest of their lives.

As rich and powerful as he was, there was nothing he could do to stop this train now that it was in motion. All he could do was recovery and damage control.

They would need to renegotiate. He would

need to increase her security, and he was going to have to move up the date of the press conference.

With a little more time to sit with the information, it was obvious to him that he had been wrong to even consider postponement at the news.

With Rita's announcement, his worst nightmare was coming to life, and in a world like that, there was no room for men like his father to have power.

And in the meantime, he would keep watch over Rita himself, here in the palace, with the support of additional security.

Soon he would have the kind of obligation in the world that he would be willing to die for. He would not allow any harm to come to it.

But she didn't have to worry about any of that now. No, he would make sure she was happy, healthy and well—the most supported pregnant woman on earth. He owed her that much for his part in things, and for the fact that she was the future mother of his child.

Lifting from his kneel, he rose, loosening his shirt and sliding into bed beside her.

Her body was stiff, resentments and tension still lingering in her muscles. He had done this to her. Fortunately, since everything else had crumbled around them, he knew a way to make it right.

As if she could sense the shifts in him, she

gazed at him, her brown eyes like two deep wells. Her lips were parted, plump and the prettiest pink, and he'd held back and punished them both for so long.

He caught her lips with a growl, and she melted into him, and he set about easing her stress one of the best ways he knew how.

She would have questions tomorrow, and he would not only have answers, he would have come up with entirely new ways to keep her out of his heart.

For both of their sakes.

CHAPTER FOURTEEN

As MUCH AS she had wanted this, as many times as she had imagined it, only to just once again curse him for being stubborn and foolish, Rita could taste the edge of panic in Jag's kiss and knew that this was not the way.

He had been so infuriating, and yet it had also all been so obviously fear.

She understood it. She felt it, too.

This wasn't what they had planned.

If making love in the moonlight had not made it clear to him that things had changed past the point of insisting they remain the same, then this certainly had.

She imagined it was hard for a man as powerful as he was to accept things not going according to plan.

But the unexpected could be good. It could have a silver lining.

They were not and would not be in love—Rita could accept that with only a mild tightness in her chest—but they cared about each other, and now they were going to have a baby. They could still be a family. They had to be, because there was no other family she had to offer to their child.

But she knew better than to present it that way to Jag.

She didn't know how she knew it, but she had sensed it the moment Jag was hers again. Just as she realized that in this moment, the lead was hers to take.

Fortunately, she was no longer new to all of it—not the palace, not the man and not the passion that flared between them—and she knew exactly what she wanted.

Bringing her hands up to cup his jaw, rather than explore the broad planes of his chest that virtually begged her to grab hold and climb on up, she gently took the reins of their kiss and told him in a different way.

And only when his own hands reached for her body, their gentle and smooth exploration tempting her to hand things back over and let him ravish her, did she take their kiss deeper.

For the second time in her life she kissed the same man, and just like the first, the experience of it threatened to carry her away.

But she wasn't going to just let them go where the wind took them.

He had given up on something tonight. His plans had collapsed, and their futures had changed.

But if the future was not what they had thought it would be, Rita could at least show him the silver lining.

They were the silver lining. This was.

They didn't have to profess love in order to build a good life together. They'd both learned the hard way the meaning of unconditional love. They could both give that to their child without having it for each other.

And they could give each other companionship and conversation and, after long last, family.

She could be happy with that if he could. Happier even than she might have been two years from now, had the terms of their original deal come to fruition.

Trailing her hands down along his jawline and neck, over his shoulders, she followed the lines of his arms all the way down to interlace her fingers with his before softly breaking the kiss.

"Come with me," she whispered, her voice only slightly uncertain until he nodded.

He hadn't wanted a family, but as she'd lived in his childhood home, she had realized that in many ways, he no longer recalled what family was.

And so tonight, she took him to the baths.

Rafida had told her he'd spent so much time in them as a boy that they'd joked he was half merman.

Since she'd been in Hayat, he had not even

visited them once. The memories of his mother, she realized now, were too strong there. And how could she not be? The baths were as much her art as cars were Rita's.

Upon realizing their destination, a rapid-fire series of emotions crossed Jag's face. Joy, pain and something more complicated came and went almost as soon as Rita had identified them.

Feeling as if their roles from the night of the debut had reversed, she squeezed his hand in the doorway, telling him without words that she believed he could do this—not just go into the baths, but be a father and not lose himself to the process.

Though his spine remained as upright as ever and the embers of his eyes burned as strong, she had never seen him so unmoored. A voice inside told her that she had the capacity to be his anchor if she dared.

An anchor did not need to be in love, so she dared.

Releasing his hand, she looked him in the eye as she reached up to slide the nightgown she wore off her shoulders.

Beneath it, she had on only a pair of panties, simple and plain, but it didn't matter. Clothes were armor for the outside world. Tonight their challenge was intimacy.

The baths provided the perfect environment.

Filled with low amber lighting that set off the

glow in his eyes, the baths consisted of multiple pools of water in various sizes and at various temperatures.

Like the rest of the palace, the design of the room showed its age with grace. In this room, that meant that traces of the seventies lingered in the amorphous shapes and overall lagoon impression of the pools, as well as in the large tropical plants that had had plenty of time to grow and mature over the years beneath their glass ceiling and accent walls.

Water permeated even the air in this room, a far cry from the setting in which they had first made love.

Rita slid her simple underwear over her hips and then stood naked before her fully clothed husband. This, too, was different from their night on the ruins.

Then he had been bare before her. Tonight she bared herself for him.

He stared without words, the fires in his eyes dancing and flickering in the gentle lighting of the room.

In this space, mirrors had been strategically placed to make both the room and foliage seem somehow bigger and deeper, but they had also been positioned so as not to reflect the bodies of anyone who might be enjoying the pools. Her display was for his eyes alone.

As always, they burned, but the fire within

them now was of an intensity that put even his normal inferno to shame.

She didn't know how long they stood like that, him fully clothed, lighting her ablaze with only the caress of his gaze, while she stood completely naked before him, but her instinct to be patient paid off when he drew her to him with a growl.

He took her mouth with need but care, his kiss nothing like the tender, reverent things he'd bestowed upon her atop the ruins.

Whereas before he had been delicate, now he was fire and force, but controlled.

Fearless, she met him head-on, exploring his mouth with her tongue as he explored hers, running her hands along his clothed body even as he ran his along her bare one.

And when she finally grew impatient with his progress in removing his attire, she simply took over the job herself, deftly releasing buttons as their tongues danced.

Only when he was naked did she break their kiss, and only then to see him in full, illuminated by the glow of the bath lights.

When she began to lead him to a warm pool, however, he shook his head, apparently tired of following. Now he was in charge, and the pool he led them to was hotter and larger than the one she had selected.

He was in a mood, and who could blame him? Years of planning had gone down the drain. But without knowing where the knowledge came from, Rita knew she had what it took to shake him out of it.

The recipe wasn't secret or complicated. He just needed her.

Or her body, at least.

How she knew when she was an utter novice on the subject wasn't important. What mattered was giving him what he needed—whether that was to lead or follow.

The heat of the pool provided a fascinating contrast as they stepped in.

The water lapping around their thighs added another layer of sensation to the exploration of their hands and mouths, and Rita moaned as the combination thrilled her senses.

Capturing her mouth again, his kisses grew in intensity, building as his frustrations funneled themselves into the kind of handling reserved for off-roading.

No matter the terrain, it seemed, the man could drive.

Cupping her breasts in his hands, he nibbled and sucked his way toward her nipples, licking and kissing the sensitive flesh along the way, and by the time he'd reached the hard buds, her breath was fast and shallow and she was arching her spine, curving to give him greater access.

"Do you like it when I touch you like this, Rita?" he asked, voice low and harsh, and she could only offer a moan in response, bringing her hands to his shoulders, trying to steady herself against a storm that came from inside.

"You're going to love the rest even more," he promised.

In the moonlight, he had been the epitome of the tender lover. Here in the baths he made her want to bite and scratch.

She was surprised to realize how much she liked it both ways.

In the relatively short time that they'd known each other, he'd already shown her so much that had been a mystery to her.

It was almost unbelievable to her that there was anything she could give in return. But at the same time, as he gripped and held, kissing her neck and doing things to her sensitive breasts that threatened to push her over the edge, she sensed that she remained the steady one.

She was the calm at the center of his storm, and she could take whatever he threw at her.

He pleasured her as if it were a competitive sport, driving her mercilessly to and over the edge multiple times with his fingers and mouth before finally lifting her up to wrap her legs around his hips in a shameless straddle.

Holding her weight with one muscled arm, he positioned himself at her entrance with his other hand, teasing and caressing her before finally sliding in.

Her moans echoed around the humid room, their sound warped and changed by the water in the air, mingling with the rhythmic sound of their bodies contacting each other's and their panting breaths.

The combination of it all, the sensual overload intertwined with their locking bodies, was enough to thrust her to climax yet again, ripping through her with enough force to carry him along for the journey, and their final primal groans happened in sync, before they both collapsed, sinking into the warm relief of the pool.

For a long time, neither of them spoke, both seeming to understand that with what had changed between them, words were just not quite enough.

Planned or not, they were well and truly partners now, committed to each other in a way neither of them had anticipated or agreed to.

And if it wasn't exactly what either of them had wanted when they set out, if their baths session had just reaffirmed anything, it was the fact that they could certainly make it work, and even feel good doing it.

CHAPTER FIFTEEN

MARRIAGE, AS RITA'S mother had explained to her, was a long twisting road, filled with unseen curves as well as massive hills and valleys—and that turned out to be true even for a fake turned not-so-fake one.

Ing took real residence in the palace alongside Rita, accompanied by an inordinate number of new security professionals. He insisted that it was simply that she was unused to the size and scope of his full retinue, but she could not recall ever seeing that many guards around him.

Along a similar vein, his arrival had also apparently necessitated an upgrade to the palace alarm system, which had been completed within the first week.

Sharing the palace, they had each fallen into individual daytime routines until their paths converged at the dinner table—which, due to Rita's new sensibilities, had become much simpler affairs.

And then, more nights than not, they shared a bed, making love and falling asleep.

And they didn't talk about any of it, not their arrangement, not their expectations, not their future.

But as much as she didn't know what to make of it, she wasn't exactly unhappy.

Jag was an attentive expecting partner, doting and involved, if not romantic, and if he was getting a little haggard and going a little overboard in terms of security, she had read that some expecting parents got that way.

He would settle down once the baby arrived. It was certainly making its presence known in every conceivable way.

Hovering on the cusp of fourteen weeks now, not only had her breasts increased in size—as most resources predicted—but her abdomen as well, the famous bump appearing rather shockingly around the twelve-week mark and having only grown since.

The same resources suggested that that was unexpected.

But she felt wonderful. Her current project—the plane Jag had promised—was flourishing, and she was alive, and steadily cared for in the company of other people in a way she had not been for a long time. As unlikely as it had all seemed in the beginning, she was going to have a family.

That was what was important. Not love, but a happy family in which no one expected anyone to be anyone that they weren't.

Overall, though she still was plagued by occasional nausea, she generally felt like a flower in bloom.

A hothouse flower hidden away from the harsh light of day and the prying eyes of people, but a flower nonetheless.

In fact, the only drawback over the past few weeks had been the intensity with which Jag was treating the effort to hide her pregnancy.

He was leaving the palace less and less and had stopped taking outside meetings.

In fact, though she was fourteen weeks pregnant and showing, she had only seen a doctor once, in part due to Jag's paranoia.

The only doctor that Jag trusted had been dealing with family matters abroad. Jag would allow no one else to know of Rita's condition. The doctor, who had made the initial house call to confirm the pregnancy and pronounce Rita exceptionally healthy before going abroad, vowed to return as soon as possible.

"As soon as possible" had still not arrived, though.

The ultrasound machine that they had tersely reminded Jag that he would need to purchase if he was going to insist that Rita never go to the clinic or hospital for care, had, however, arrived.

And the doctor was due next week.

Soon, she would see her baby for the first time.

And in the meantime, she had days filled with adjusting her work to her pregnancy and Jag.

The thought filled her with a sense of well-being. Even if things remained the way they had ended with her family of origin, Rita had found herself a family after all.

A week later, however, Rita was forced to reevaluate her sentiments as she looked at the brand-spanking-new three-dimensional ultrasound image that showed she was carrying not just one baby, but two.

"Well, that answers why you're so huge!" the doc said with a chuckle. "I didn't want to alarm anyone, but I was already considering the conditions that could have resulted in that…" The sentence trailed off as the hand moving the wand around in the mess of jelly on Rita's abdomen stopped. "Oh, and there's the smaller one again. Such healthy babies. Of course, healthy or no, this being a twin pregnancy means the risk is higher. That is just a fact. Therefore, you must be even more vigilant about eating right and getting proper exercise and sunlight. Not too much stress either, and no harsh chemicals. You may need to take a hiatus from your garage, Princess, and—"

Jag cut them off impatiently with the words, "What do you mean, healthy or not? How can she be healthy and high-risk at the same time? That makes no sense."

Shrugging with a knowing smile aimed at the Prince, the doctor replied, "Twice the baby, twice the potential for complications, twice the development that could go wrong, twice the baby to safely deliver. A singleton pregnancy requires a woman to operate at the height of human endurance for months at a time. A woman carrying two babies is doing double that. But do not worry, my prince, our princess here is healthy and strong and so clever that I bet she'll think of a brand-new way to deliver entirely."

The doctor gave parting advice and left. Rita placed a cool palm on Jag's thigh. "I can handle this."

For a moment, he did not reply. She wondered if he was so lost in his worries that he had not even heard her speak. But then he smiled, kissed her forehead and said, "I have no doubt."

CHAPTER SIXTEEN

THE PRESS CONFERENCE had been moved up and his palace made as secure as it was possible to be with a fully functioning home office and the comings and goings of his staff, but Jag felt helpless.

How was he supposed to keep Rita and his children safe from his father, conduct his work, and keep her stress levels healthy for the next four months? And after that?

He couldn't do it here.

Rita didn't know it, but his father had been becoming increasingly aggressive in his attempts to breach the protective ring of security that Jag had established around her since the announcement of their marriage.

He had already attempted to get to her multiple times, and that was without even knowing she was carrying the future of the family line. Both of them.

Twice the baby, twice the risk.

He had to get Rita and their children out of

his father's reach entirely—had to make sure they were literally and physically outside of the range of a man who had already shown Jag that he wasn't above using any means necessary, and then he needed to get rid of the threat altogether.

Even here, with his near-constant presence at her side and within the palace that had been built to ensure privacy and security, they were not protected enough.

Nothing could happen to them; he would not be able to function.

He trusted Rafida and his security team with his life.

He trusted no one but Rita with the life of his children.

And that meant there was only one option.

She wouldn't like it, but there was only one place on earth that he could trust to be completely out of the reach of his father, one place where he could be certain that Rita and their babies would be safe.

"Pack your things," he told her when he found her in her garage, his voice implacable and firm, before adding, "We leave in an hour," and no further explanation.

There would be plenty of time to explain everything on their journey there, and she would have the rest of her pregnancy to come around to understanding exactly why they had to go.

This was their only option.

Rita claimed to understand the risk she was in, but she didn't truly. She thought Jag was over-reacting, because she had never truly had to deal with a man as ruthless and distanced from healthy bonds of love as his father was.

That was what made everything that his father had done to him so particularly twisted. His father had undertaken everything that he'd done to Jag and his mother in the name of love.

From the day of his birth, Jag had been his father's pride and joy. Unfortunately, his father had long ago confused love with control.

He loved his perfect son; he just happened to see no problem in using psychological warfare to ensure that perfection.

He never beat his son—he'd simply played a lifetime of mind games, surveilling him and monitoring all of his relationships in order to in-fluence his behavior.

When bribery didn't work, he resorted to more menacing and long-term solutions, such as sepa-rating him from his mother and sending him to boarding school.

Nothing like that would ever happen to either of his children.

He would get his family to safety and then he would return and deal with his father once and for all.

Now that he knew he was becoming the fa-ther of not one but two souls, that he would be beholden to two beings who could run in opposite directions while he struggled to keep them safe, one thing was absolutely clear to him: the time for subtlety had ended.

Hayat had a room for only one ruler, and his name was Jahangir Hassan Umar Al Hayat.

The moment of his ascendancy had arrived—Rita's life and his children's lives depended on it.

All hail King Jag.

He'd given her less than an hour, which was hardly enough time to carefully pack the drapey new wardrobe pieces that Jameel had created for her under the guise of making her loungewear.

Without time for even a lingering goodbye to her fleet, she rushed through the palace garage that was now home to her fleet on the way to the Mercedes touring van that would take them to their mystery destination.

The vehicle suggested it might be a long drive.

Under normal circumstances, Rita would be looking forward to it. But newly aware that she carried twins and was saddled with a paranoid husband, the whole thing lacked adventurous appeal.

It seemed there was a limit even to her patented brand of recklessness.

And yet here she was, following the lead of her husband.

The father of her children.

Not *child*, as she'd spent the past weeks cooing, but *children*.

Had one of them been feeling left out this whole time?

Suddenly, she felt as paranoid as her husband, but for fear that she had already begun failing as a mother and had not yet even met her children.

But beyond protective, how did *he* feel about the news? Was he happy?

She didn't know. She knew only that he was resolute and certain of a next move that he still hadn't let her in on.

It was, indeed, a long trip—long enough that she was grateful that the tour van had a bathroom. She hadn't known it was possible for a human to need to use the restroom so many times in one day.

Jag had been silent and broody as he drove through the first still-dark hours of their journey, and while she had had every intention of forcing him to talk, the combination of the late hour and the smooth motion of the van and her pregnant state made her fall asleep.

When she woke, the sun was close to setting and they were driving on an otherwise empty road in a stretch of bleached-out desert without a thing in sight.

Her husband's aura appeared no less inclined

to talk, but now she had daylight and alertness on her side.

"Where are we going?" she asked, for not the first time.

Miraculously, this time he answered. "My mother's oasis."

The image of date palms clustered around a small pond in the sand filled her mind, but it didn't fit with her sense of Jag's tastes. "Your mother's oasis?"

The nearing twilight brought another miracle with it—he smiled.

And as much as she wished she could be immune and unmoved, seeing him crack—even if it was just one corner of his mouth lifting—made her heart beat faster.

"It's not what you're picturing," he said, reading her mind, as always.

"Then what is it?" she asked.

"My mother's family had land at the far western point of Hayat. By appearances, it is a wasteland of sand, far off the beaten path of traditional nomadic routes," he said.

Catching his drift, she said, "But appearances can be deceiving?"

Nodding, the other corner of his mouth joining the first to bring a real, full smile to his lips, he said, "They can, indeed. The land has been in my mother's family for generations, its true worth kept as a cherished secret in order to preserve and protect it. It was a wise move. Because she kept the secret even from her husband, she was able to leave it to me when she died and my father, thinking it useless and valueless, had no incentive to steal it. And when I came of age, I made sure it was no longer possible."

"But really there's an oasis there?" she asked.

"Not naturally. But naturally, there is groundwater. Lots and lots of it. Formed by a large underground porous stone system, in the desert, it is more priceless than gold. My family found the water by chance. They built, maintained and kept secret the oasis, by choice."

"And you couldn't tell me when we were at home because of the secret."

He nodded.

"I thought you trusted Rafida," she said softly, a hand coming to her abdomen.

Jag's face went hard. "I do. You, however, are the only person I've ever trusted with this. Our family has managed the water for hundreds of years, going so far as to engage in a state-of-the-art catchment to refresh from what little rain we get. This is not mere wealth, but survival."

"Is it abandoned, then?" she asked.

Shoulders loosening, he gave his head a brief shake. "No. There is an entire village responsible for managing, monitoring and protecting it."

"Protecting it?" she prodded, picturing armed soldiers in fatigues.

"It's water in the desert, Rita."

So her picture might not be that far off.

"And it's very remote?"

He nodded. "As remote as you can get and still be in Hayat."

"And why are we going?"

"It's the only place I can be sure the twins and you will be safe from my father."

Flatly, she said, "Well, thanks for telling me."

"Everything's changed now," he countered. "It's one thing to take responsibility for the safety of an adult woman who can consent to a certain level of risk. It's another to protect a woman pregnant with twins from a man who would not think twice about threatening his unborn grandchildren if it meant controlling me."

Again, her hand came to shield their growing babies. "I see."

"Do you?" he pressed, temper fraying. "Do you see what has to be done?"

Rita's eyebrows came together. She understood that the threat they were facing was graver than she had initially imagined, but she did not see how that led them to driving to a secret oasis in the remote desert.

"I'm taking you to Jana to stay there for the remainder of your pregnancy. It is the only place I can be assured of your safety. My father cannot get to you in a place he does not know exists."

"What?" Rita shrieked, her hand coming down to grip the armrest at her side.

Jag remained calm, despite her outburst. "I am taking you to the oasis for your pregnancy," he repeated calmly.

"No," Rita said.

Jag kept his eyes on the road. "We're already halfway there."

"I don't care. Turn the car around."

"No," Jag said.

She crossed her arms in front of her chest. "Then you're kidnapping me."

He shrugged, the move incredibly American. "So be it."

Dropping her arms, she smashed her fist against the armrest. "Not so be it. You can't kidnap me."

"It seems I already have. And I seem to recall you packing your own bags and getting into the car willingly."

Narrowing her eyes, a new suspicion forming in her mind, she asked, "And what are you going to be doing?"

Brushing her question off, he said, "Everything I normally do, in Hayat City. I would stay with you, but I cannot. Not if I hope to keep it a secret. People are already remarking that they have seen very little of me of late. Your retreat from the public is one thing, but a prince cannot disappear for six months. My responsibilities require my presence in the capital."

She hissed in response, and he took a sudden left, veering the vehicle onto a steep, hidden road to a hidden rocky valley, nestled in the folds of which was a cozy oasis lagoon and town.

Under any other circumstances, Rita would have been thrilled at the sight of the lush, beautiful surprise, lit up by a colorful sunset, but at the current moment, she would have been happy to burn it all down with a glare.

Glorious water that went from blue-green at its shallows to deep turquoise at its depths pooled in the large, long lagoon that was surrounded by rocky outcrops on one side and a tidy adobe village built into the surrounding hillsides on the other.

While most of the structures in the village looked ancient, there were modern buildings mixed in among the old.

Few cars dotted its roads, and most of them were parked.

Figures moved about on the streets, but from this distance it wasn't possible to tell if they were men or women, adults or children.

"The hospital in the village is brand-new and staffed with excellent practitioners whom I personally selected to service the people that live here. For all of its isolation, you will not lack quick medical care."

Rita could not help but be blown away, not by the advancement of this remote village—which was impressive—but by her husband's ability to simply charge forward as if they were not in the middle of an active argument, and he was not in the midst of depositing her like so much trash in the desert.

"I'm sure there's a library, too," she said sarcastically.

"As a matter of fact," he said tersely, "there is."

"How convenient for me."

He said nothing to that.

Curving their way out of the village around a long bend, the landscape opened up to reveal a gorgeous massive stone fortress. From size alone she would have guessed that this was the familial home of the rulers of this isolated microcommunity.

Outside of it, gorgeous foliage softened the stone facade, naturally blending into the surrounding landscape, and if she wasn't mistaken, there were frankincense trees mixed in with the date palms and shrubs.

To the right of the grand stone palace was another open lagoon, deep and still and clear, its mirror finish so crystalline and reflective that Rita would not have been surprised to look into its depths and see all the way to the center of the Earth.

Stopping the Mercedes in front of the timeless structure, Jag said, "We're here."

"I'm not getting out of the car, Jag."

"Then I'll carry you."

"Then do it," she challenged, not exactly understanding the energy that washed over her but willing to let it take the lead. Perhaps it was pregnancy.

Or perhaps it was that she was tired of being dictated to by tyrannical men.

Whatever it was, Rita had reached her limit as far as being pushed around went.

He could listen to her dictate things for a change. "You can drag me kicking and screaming and leave me here and no one will be the wiser. But you and I will know, and neither of us will forget the wrong you were willing to commit against me because of your own fear and pride. This single action will fester between us until our relationship deteriorates because you know it's wrong."

"Fear and pride? You think this is about fear and pride? You think it was fear and pride that led me to drive you all the way out here? To share one of my family's oldest secrets with you? To do everything in my power to keep you happy and safe and satisfied? Look around you, Rita. I'm doing all of this because I love you." He hadn't raised his voice, not truly, but shouted the last, nonetheless.

Rita's eyes widened, her head shaking back and forth in denial.

"It's true, Rita. I love you. It all ended for me the night in the ruins. Before that. When you stood up to my father at the finale and I realized that you weren't merely the ideal woman for my aims, but the ideal woman for me. You shine as my partner, my queen and already as the mother of my children. You're everything I will ever want. I must know that you and the babies are safe from my father. It's not forever, Rita. Just until I've taken care of my father. I just need this peace of mind. If you can't do it for the babies, if you can't believe me about my father, do it for me. I love you, Rita."

He said it a second time, his voice lighter, as if he felt better in the telling, while Rita stared at him in horror, mouthing the word *no*.

"No," she finally voiced, when sound came through her throat. "No," she repeated. "No, Jag. No. No. No. Don't do this. Don't ask this of me. Don't make my family contingent on bending to your will. Don't tell me you love me while you're demanding I sacrifice myself to your needs. Don't you do this to me, too, Jag. I thought you were different."

Color draining from his face, Jag raised his palms as if to stop her from going on, from taking the train of thought any further, but it was too late.

"Don't be my father, Jag," she begged, adding, "Don't be yours."

Fire flashed through his eyes, but Rita didn't look away. She'd meant every word she said. If he left her here, right now, she would never forgive him.

"Rita, that's not what I meant…" he began, but she shook her head. There was only one thing she wanted to hear from him, and it wasn't excuses.

It was that they were going back to Hayat City.

She had a right to stand up for herself; facing off with her husband in the desert, she realized the truth of that.

She had always had a right to stand up for herself. With Jag, and with her father, so long ago.

She wasn't the one who had been in the wrong all those years ago—her father had been. She had been young and willful, but Jag had been right. She had also been a loyal testament to her family. The transgression of staying true to the passion that had taken her so far was not one that was worthy of losing her family.

Just as the transgression of being pregnant with twins was not worthy of twiddling her thumbs in the far reaches of the desert. She was healthy and strong and would stay that way only if she had the space and freedom to keep both mind and body occupied. She needed her workdays in her garage and her dinners and nights with Jag.

She didn't need to be hidden away in a desert tower—no matter how beautiful an oasis it was.

Like Jag was now, her father had overreacted and overreached. Back then, she had been too young to do anything about it.

Today, she was a grown woman carrying twins.

Jag blinked and looked away.

Staring around him at the astounding architecture of the Jana palace, he cleared his throat. Then he got back into the van.

Rita didn't crow in triumph, because there was no triumph in learning that her husband was not above using the same techniques as her father, but she took comfort in the fact that at the very least, this time she hadn't stood for it.

CHAPTER SEVENTEEN

JAG DROVE BACK to Hayat City with Rita in tow because she was right.

He could have easily left her there, confident in her safety and security, and in doing so, would have become just like her father, demanding she bend in the name of his love.

He could not believe he had confessed to her as he had done. The frantic moments between acknowledging it himself and throwing it at her the way he had was matched only by the poor quality of his delivery.

And yet avoiding that slippery slope brought Jag no closer to a solution regarding what to do to keep Rita safe from the man.

It had only left him outside her good graces.

It was ironic that the things he had so feared—falling for Rita, having children with her—in the end had paled in comparison to the damage he had done simply by speaking.

And yet as bumbling as he had been in his

communications with Rita, he knew he was right to not shake his concern regarding his father.

He would sort things out with her later, in the lifetime they had ahead them, even if it meant he had to spend the whole of it making her fall in love with him.

His father he would deal with now.

In T minus ten minutes.

In moments, he would go on national television and bring shame to his family name. He hoped he would also restore honor to it, taking his father down in the process.

The space between the conclusion of his broadcast and his father's arrest would likely be the most dangerous for Rita and the children, and he had doubled palace perimeter security to coincide with the timing.

He had told Rita—she refused to go anywhere safer, of course, but Rafida was to send him updates regarding his wife's status.

No updates had arrived, but he had sent in the extra guard after waiting a generous amount of time anyway.

He wanted her and their children safe.

Twenty-seven minutes later, the same number as Rita's age, Jag noted, he stepped out of the bright television lighting and offstage.

Like his exhibition, the broadcast had gone off with a hitch.

The grand finale of his plan had been set in motion.

There was no telling how far his desperate and enraged father might be willing to go until the special services caught up with him, but his reign of manipulation and control was over.

Unfortunately, the answer arrived a few moments later, with the message that came through from the head of security.

Rita had stepped out for a moment of air in the courtyard and disappeared.

They were searching for her, the team leader assured Jag, but he could have told them not to bother.

He knew where she would be, and what he would have to do to get her back.

CHAPTER EIGHTEEN

FOR THE SECOND time in her life, Rita was face-to-face with her father-in-law.

As far as evil villains went, her father-in-law appeared frail and weak.

But as he had just successfully kidnapped her from her own home despite a crack security team, she recognized that it was probably time to revise her opinion.

Long past, really.

She also recognized that she had perhaps taken the threat he presented for granted.

She had not truly believed the man could be cruel enough to harm his own grandchildren. She could admit that to herself now, as she was uncomfortably tied to a chair in the center of his private balcony.

Admitting that also meant admitting that perhaps Jag had meant what he said when he tried to leave her at Jana, and that it might actually have been the only place he could think of that would be safe for her and their children.

Of course, while these were important truths to discover, they paled in comparison to the necessity of escape.

Her babies were depending on her.

"So this is why he disappeared with his whore," her father-in-law said, stroking the thin beard that graced his chin, eyeing her growing bump.

But hiding her pregnancy was no longer her top priority. Keeping her babies alive and getting away from her father-in-law was.

And though she didn't have an escape plan yet, she did have the wherewithal to engage in one of the oldest strategies in the book: stalling.

If she could get him talking and keep him talking, she might buy herself enough time to figure out a way out.

"I am not a whore," she retorted.

Making a face at her oversharing, the old king scoffed, saying, "Everyone knows American girls are easy. You may have fooled my son, but you will never fool me. And you have brought as much shame on my house as I will allow. My son has done me a favor in hiding your pregnancy. No one need know more than the fact that you died in a tragic accident. As a widower, my son can make a more appropriate selection for his next wife."

The idea of Jag with another woman was a knife in her chest, but she would not let this cruel man see it.

"You know what?" Rita said. "I'm getting real tired of everyone talking about what's wrong with me."

Taken aback, her father-in-law looked mildly surprised and confused, as if perhaps he thought she might not have heard the words he'd said.

Taking advantage of the pause, she jumped back in with, "It's always how my interests are not the right ones, nor my choices, nor passions. First it was my father, and now you, each one telling me that I am somehow inappropriate, that I need to change to better fit your image of the world. Well, you know what," she said. "I'm tired of it. And it was your son who made me see it. Never once has he asked me to change who I am to better fit his requirements. He delights in who I am, without alteration or revision, and I have been a fool to not realize what a precious gift that kind of love is. Unconditional. It is something you will never understand, so I won't waste my breath trying to explain, but I will not allow you to call me a whore. I am no man's whore, but I am your son's wife. I will be the mother of his children and your grandchildren, and what is more than that, I love him and them with every fiber of my being. I will not tolerate you disrespecting what we have built. I was accepted to the University of California at Berkeley at the age of sixteen. At the age of eighteen my father cut me off in one of the most expensive cities in the world and not only did I manage to pay for my life with my work, I also paid for the remainder of my tuition. By the age of twenty, I had a dual master's degree in computer science and mechanical engineering, as well as a start-up valued at two million dollars. And while I don't expect you to be impressed with that kind of money, I do expect you to be impressed by the fact that seven years later I had invented multiple technologies with the capacity to change the world. Interest in Hayat has skyrocketed since the world found out about its new American Bengali Muslim working-class princess, and your son is the most popular royal your line has seen in generations. By my calculations, I'd say that means your reign is coming to a close, and, in addition to being absolutely suitable to be a princess exactly as I am, I am exceptional at math."

She was under no impression that her little speech would inspire her father-in-law to release her; it was merely a way to eat some time and release a bit of righteous indignation and fear she felt.

So she was surprised when, as soon as she finished speaking, a massive commotion erupted at the entrance to the room, and like an ancient warrior, Jag flew in.

Seeing him, knowing he knew where she was and trusting him entirely to get her and their babies safely out of there, she surprised herself by bursting into tears.

She and her babies had narrowly escaped disaster.

And she wouldn't have to do the rest on her own.

She was ready to tell him now how desperately in love she had fallen with him. Having been brave enough to say it out loud once, she was ready to do it again for real with him.

She had finally learned to speak up for herself and to fight for what she loved—people, places and things.

She was brave enough to own her emotions, her hopes, her dreams and her actions.

And because of that, she could demand the same of others, including her parents.

Jag had been her safe space and testing ground for the theory, and once he'd taken care of things here and they were in a bit safer a spot and she'd had a chance to shower him with her declarations of love, she vowed to take everything that she'd learned and make her family listen, too.

CHAPTER NINETEEN

JAG HAD DRIVEN from his palace directly to his father's, where he knew Rita would be.

Arriving there, he took the stairs two at a time before sprinting toward his father's private chambers, in time to hear Rita, strident and proud, declare to his father that she loved him and their babies and she would tolerate no disrespect on the matter.

As if he had sprouted wings at her words, he tore through the distance to find what was truly his nightmare come to life, all of this familiar as much as it was new.

Falling in love with Rita and getting her pregnant had not been the nightmare. His father was.

Seeing his father standing before his wife, who was tied up in a chair and crying, was a real nightmare.

His father intended to throw her off the balcony.

Jag was as certain of it as he was of his own name. The man who had consigned Jag's mother to die alone would not hesitate to throw the woman he loved and their unborn children off a balcony. His father loved his power positions, and his private balcony had always been his favorite.

Jag did not think, plan or strategize. Impossibly, he simply sped up—running at his father and Rita far faster than the pace of his father's deranged retreat.

With a roar, he leaped, reaching out to clasp Rita's wrist with an iron grip before swinging his body to kick his father away from her, catching the man in the chest.

His father flew backward, but as soon as Rita was free from his grasp, Jag had no more attention for the man. Law enforcement had been quick on Jag's heels; they would deal with his father.

Instead, all of his focus landed on his wife.

"Are you hurt?" Jag asked her, frantically checking her arms and legs where the ropes chafed against her skin.

Rita shook her head. "No. Not even scared now that you're here."

"I'm not sure your confidence isn't misplaced, but I'm grateful for it," he said.

"Spare me the romantic reunion," his father croaked from the floor behind them, where he had pushed himself to his feet. "Your bride and I were just discussing the happy news."

"You have nothing to discuss with my bride," Jag said coldly, "now or ever."

His father clucked his tongue at him. "Now, is that any way to speak with the father who loves you?"

Rather than engage his father in his games, though, once again, Jag turned his back on the old man, giving his attention instead to his wife. "Let's get these ropes off you, shall we?" he said to her.

"You will look at me when I speak to you. I am your father and you will love and respect me," his father warned ominously. "Dammit, Jahangir, look at me. Your king addresses you!"

But Jag did not turn.

Instead, he worked on the ropes that held Rita in place.

Only when she was free did he address his father, finally turning to look at him with nothing but pity in his eyes.

"I neither love nor respect you, Father, and your days as King have come to an end."

Scoffing, his father said, "Youthful defiance and arrogance."

But Jag shook his head. "I'm afraid not, Father. I have just finished debriefing the people of Hayat on the collection of information and evidence I have put together to depose you a thousand times over. You are not my king, nor the people's king, and you ceased to be my father a long time ago. You will be tried and punished through the legal system according to your crimes, and it will take the people some time to rebuild their faith and trust in the royal family, which they will because of my and my wife's efforts, but you, you will never rule again."

Choking on his own rage spittle, the old King sputtered, "You will never sleep again, knowing I am out there, plotting."

Rita sucked in a quiet gasp, but Jag held firm. "I know you will try. I just won't be losing any sleep over it. It's finished. I should have ended this a long time ago. You're going to prison, Dad."

As if the drama were being staged rather than lived in real life, the authorities chose that moment to finally make their entrance, converging on the former King to arrest him.

But Jag had no time or attention for his father any longer.

Pulling Rita into his arms, he held her to him as closely as her enormous belly would allow, pressing desperate kisses on the top of her head, grateful to press her into the safety of his arms.

Only when he heard her muffled "Jag, I can't breathe" did he release her from the lock of his hold, and even then, only wide enough to allow her to pull back a fraction.

"How did he get to you?" he demanded when she did.

Smiling, her eyes filled with tears again. "It

was just like you warned me. It was like getting jumped by a bunch of ninjas, rappelling in from the roof."

Shaking his head, he said, "I'm sorry, Rita. I broke my promise. I didn't keep you safe."

Wrapping her arms around his neck, her embrace delicate yet strong, she said, "Oh, Jag. You tried. I just didn't listen. You were right about Jana. I'm sorry I was too headstrong to see that."

Pulling back to look at her, he shook his head. "No, Rita. You were right. It wasn't right to ask you to hem yourself in because I could not handle how much being in love with you, loving our children, terrifies me. I am so sorry you had to experience this, but there is one thing I am grateful for—a silver lining, if you will."

"What is it?" she asked.

"Who knows how long it would have taken you to calm down enough to admit you were in love with me if we'd just stayed home?" he teased.

But this time, she did not match his energy.

Instead, the tears left in her eyes spilled over and she swiped at them quickly, never losing her smile. "I know I wasn't supposed to, but I love you, Jag. More than even planes, trains and automobiles."

He closed his eyes and drew in a long, deep breath, pressing his forehead to hers, letting the warmth and completion of her words roll over and dig into him. "Thank you for loving me, Rita.

I am sorry for running from you and trying to control you. Love had been absent in my life so long that I feared both its return and then the risk of its loss again. I love you, Rita. More than life itself."

Beaming like sun, her tears flowing freely, Jag had the strangest thought that she might sprout a rainbow.

It would be only fitting. A storm had passed, after all.

"You're going to be an amazing king," she said.

A half smile on his face, he said to her, "And you will be my queen."

EPILOGUE

APPROXIMATELY TWO MONTHS LATER, hovering around twenty-six weeks pregnant with twins, Rita stepped onto the long red aisle, but the phenomenal dress that Jameel had created for her did a remarkable job of flattering her bump.

Fitted at the neck and chest, with a high lace collar above a sheer white bodice and capelet-inspired sleeves, the skirt was full and voluminous and in combination with its illusion Empire waistline, looking direct from the front, it didn't even look like she was expecting at all. Even from the side, one might be inclined to attribute the width of the skirt to the layers of tulle and fairy-tale-princess nature of the dress.

Rita could think of nothing better for the fairy-tale ending of her and Jag's story, which, it turned out, had been a love story after all.

As they celebrated their Western-style wedding, which was to be the first of many hosted events to make up for the rushed and administerial nature of their actual wedding, Rita reveled in the joy that she had gotten everything she had ever wanted.

She had a loving partner, a family on the way, and now, just six months after the exhibition, she had even begun to change the way the world drove.

Beginning with Hayat, she had been a part of overseeing the beginning of their transition to all electric transport, and she had messages from two American and two Japanese car companies to discuss her first-ever car design that could be mass-produced waiting for her to respond to after she and Jag enjoyed their first real honeymoon.

Like their celebratory events, he had assured her that their upcoming luxury yachting trip would be just the first of many romantic getaways they would share. Each had gone too long in their lives without the comfort and warmth of regular affection and celebration, and each was committed to making it up to the other.

They were a family, full of love and laughter, but also one equipped to handle disagreement and challenge. They had faced it all and come through the other side more dedicated to each other than they had begun, and it didn't get much better than that.

Or rather, it seemed it continually got better.

They had been lucky enough to find the right partners, the kinds of people who would poke and prod and encourage until evolution occurred.

Rita was only reminded of the truth of that as she smiled at her father before looping her arm through his.

That her father would be involved in any wedding of hers was a miracle in itself. That Jag had coordinated their reconciliation in time for the televised ceremony, the kind of sweet detail she would always love him for.

He was a master at planning, though perhaps still a bit high-handed about it all, as he hadn't told her what was going on through the process, simply shoved her into a room where her father already stood. In this instance, however, she did not mind. He made her brave and forced her to go after her heart's desires.

She could not lie and say it had been easy, but when they'd passed the reticence to speak and resentment and defensiveness, Rita, now practiced in the art of speaking up for herself when she needed to, was finally able to say the thing she had needed to say all those years ago but not known she had the right to.

"I'm so sorry for what I did, Papa," she started with. "I should have never lied to you. But what you did was wrong, too, and you owe me an apology. A parent shouldn't stand in the way of their children's dreams, happiness or future. It took me a while to learn it, but now that I am going to be a parent, it is even more clear. You didn't have to agree with me, but you were supposed to love me, no matter what I did. I deserve that."

And because everything she had said was true, and because words were insufficient to address everything that had passed between them, her father had merely nodded, tears streaming down his face, and opened his arms.

Smiling through her own tears, Rita had gone into them. And after they'd hugged, they stepped back from each other to look at how the years had changed them.

Her father had looked at her enormous belly and a thousand emotions flashed across his face. Settling on a soft smile, he said, "You got pretty fat."

And Rita had snorted and said, "Your hair turned gray."

With a chuckle, her father reached a hand to pat the salt and pepper of his hair. "A lot of time has passed. Too much. I'm so sorry, my sweet Amrita. I was a fool, but I have never stopped being proud of you. You did everything you promised to do, my girl."

And it had been enough to get to this point, her father walking her down the aisle in a beautiful dress to once again marry the man she loved, this time in the presence of her mother and father, her sister, and her uncles, and the family she was growing and would protect with her life.

It was a far cry from a judge and a jumpsuit.

Eleven weeks later

Rita went into labor in the wee hours of the morning, and like everything else she did, she raced through it fast and hard.

Their twins came into the world healthy and loud, their daughter first, followed by their son.

All of Hayat rejoiced in welcoming the new Princess and Prince, particularly eager to celebrate as a conclusion to their short and sedate mourning of the death of their old king. They went all out with parades and festivities to commemorate the birth, as well as their new, already much beloved, King and Queen.

They were especially excited about the Queen.

Their babies were like mirror images of them, their son taking after Rita, bearing her big round brown eyes and button nose, while their daughter's eyes were almond-shaped and amber, and her nose long and straight.

Their son they had named Martin Hatem Kabir Al Hayat, because Martin was as close to naming a child after a car as he would allow Rita to go, and their daughter, Benazir Summar Al Hayat because Jag had been moved when he'd learned that Rita's middle name, Benazir, was the same as his mother's first.

And three more years of joyous reigning and happy marriage after that, with two rambunctious royal preschoolers—a boy who loved to go fast and a girl with a mind for strategy—Rita told Jag she that was pregnant for the second time, this time completely without hesitation or fear, and they celebrated the news with their whole family.

* * * * *